THE BOATHOUSE KILLER

NORFOLK COZY MYSTERIES

KEITH FINNEY

Keith Finney - Author

AN INVITATION

Welcome to your invitation to join my Readers' Club.

Receive free, exclusive content only available to members including short stories, character interviews and much more.

To join, click on the link towards the end of this book and you're in!

1

AFTERNOON DRINKS

Anthony Stanton's little-boy act tested Lyn Blackthorn's patience to the limit.

"What's not to like? You've got a pint of Fen Bodger, the sun's out, and the chicken burger didn't cost you a penny."

"Call yourself my best mate? You know I hate BBQs. Anyway, it isn't free. The tickets were twenty-five quid apiece."

Lyn shook her head and frowned as she scanned the lively scene in the beer garden of her favourite waterside pub, *The New Tavern*.

"I'll pay for the stupid tickets if it pains you so much, you tight devil. Anyone would think you were seven years old, not thirty-two."

She gave Ant her best head-teacher look, reserved for only the most testing of pupils.

"That's not the point. Just because you're three months older doesn't mean you can treat me like a child. I—"

Before he could finish, Lyn turned to welcome Fitch, an old friend of the pair and owner of Fitch's Automotive Services.

"Don't tell me, he's moaning about spending money again, isn't he?"

Ant frowned.

Lyn raised an eyebrow and shook her head.

"I suppose it's inbred into aristocrats like Lord Anthony Stanton here, or should I call you by your ancestral name. What is it—Norton-D'Arcy? You know what they're like, Fitch. Steal from the poor and get them to pay for your chicken burgers."

She watched as Ant refused to take the bait, stiffened his posture, and tilted his head upwards.

"Then you two should know your place in the pecking order, should you not?"

As if, thought Lyn.

Ant's cheeky reply cut no ice, and both friends dissolved into a fit of laughter.

"Oh, yes. We know our place all right, don't we, Fitch? More to the point, my lord, just at this moment *your* place is at the bar because the drinks are on you."

Lyn stifled Ant's protest with another of her head-teacher looks together with a forefinger pointing straight at the tavern's rear entrance.

"I'll have a large white wine with ice and a slice. Pint of Thatcher's Itch, Fitch?"

He nodded.

"You can have a shandy, Ant. Remember, you have a boat to sail home, and we all recall what happened the last time you had a skinful."

Lyn got the reaction she expected.

"I beg to differ. The cause of that run-in with Maynard's wreck of a boat was a faulty tiller, not Fen Bodger pale ale."

Lyn shrugged her shoulders. Fitch shook his head.

"Well, it certainly ended up a wreck when you'd finished

with it. Anyway, off to the bar you go because we're gasping for some liquid refreshment."

Shamed into paying for the round, Ant did an about turn and began to weave his way through the crowd.

Lyn caught Fitch's eye and broke out into a fit of the giggles.

"Did you sail down on *Fieldsurfer*?"

Happy as she was to continue enjoying Ant's discomfort, Lyn thought better of it and focussed on Fitch's attempt to move the conversation on.

"Yes. I took a chocolate cake to his parents. Ant suggested it might be easier to sail down Stanton Broad rather than driving through Butler's Chase. You know what it can be like at the weekend during the tourist season. Anyway, she's moored just over there."

Lyn pointed at the Earl of Stanton's, clinker-built wherry resting majestically on the Broad, standing out as she did from a line of modern fibreglass tourist hire boats.

Ant's lucky his father lets him loose with Fieldsurfer.

Just then, Lyn became aware of someone crying. Turning, she saw two women. One trying to console the other.

"None of our business, Lyn."

Men.

"Occupational habit, I'm afraid. My ears are autotuned to that particular sound."

She ambled toward the couple and sensed Fitch was close behind acting like an unhappy sibling following their mother to the dentist.

She recognised one of the women. Newly married, she'd only recently moved to the village.

"Hannah, isn't it? Can I help?"

Lyn spoke in a soft tone, making sure she gave each woman equal eye contact.

"It's fine, thank you. My friend will be okay."

She's Polish?

Lyn ignored the well-meant rebuttal and instead focused her attention on the tearful one.

"You're Hannah Singleton?"

The woman wiped a tear from her cheek.

Be careful. Don't push too hard, thought Lyn.

"Oh, don't mind me. I'm just a nosy teacher. But it does mean I get to hear what's going on in the village." Lyn smiled in a calculated move to put the woman at ease.

Hannah looked at her companion and gave a slight nod. Turning back to Lyn, she hesitated for a few seconds.

"You run the little school, yes? People have told me about you."

Lyn blushed.

"Oh dear, that bad?"

Hannah looked confused.

"No, sorry. I mean—"

Oops.

Fitch filled the awkward gap.

"No need to apologise. She's well known for being a busybody. Teachers are all the same, aren't they?"

Lyn relaxed in the knowledge Fitch's icebreaker had worked.

"This is my friend, Annabelle. We grew up in the same town. We are, how you say, best mates?"

"Just like Fitch and me."

"Am I really, Lyn?"

His smile gave the game away.

Lyn turned back to Hannah.

"I hope we yokels haven't done anything to upset you?"

Lyn's attempt at humour had the opposite effect.

Well, I got that wrong.

She watched as Hannah once more began to cry. This time, people standing nearby started to stare.

"Oh, it's not what you have said. You see, they have had their first serious argument as husband and wife, and now he is gone."

Lyn frowned, struggling to make sense of Annabelle's explanation.

"Gone? Gone where?"

Fitch fidgeted and busied himself checking his wristwatch. Lyn knew her friend didn't do emotional angst, much preferring the objectivity of cars, which either did, or did not, work. Lyn was also conscious that talk of her husband intensified Hannah's state of distress.

"I do not know what is wrong with him. Geoff said he had to go to the boathouse. I offered to go with him, but he shouted at me and rushed out of our home."

Lyn stepped closer as Hannah's voice trembled with emotion.

"Now he does not answer his mobile."

Annabelle gently placed a reassuring hand on her friend's shoulder.

"It is true. Geoff is always so patient and never loses his temper. Something is troubling him. I have noticed this for several weeks now."

That sort of talk isn't doing Hannah any good at all.

"Who's worried about what?"

The voice coming closer interrupted Annabelle's flow.

Lyn recognised it immediately.

"This brute is Anthony Stanton. You'll get used to him."

Lyn waved an arm in Ant's general direction as she introduced him. She noticed Hannah's lack of reaction, whereas Annabelle gave him a broad smile.

You're flirting with him!

"Your surname is the same as the village. Are you the earl's—"

Ant smiled.

"For my sins, yes."

Lyn gatecrashed the exchange.

"Always one for flattery, eh, my lord? If that head of yours gets any bigger, it'll explode."

"Boom."

Lyn had placed a hand on either temple to emphasise the point.

Ant looked distinctly unimpressed.

"Mock me if you wish. I care not."

The three friends giggled before Lyn turned back to Hannah, who was still crying despite their efforts to lighten the mood.

Time to sort this.

"Hannah, you bought old Kimberly's boathouse, didn't you?"

Hannah nodded.

"Ant's boat is just over there." She pointed to the wherry. "It's only ten minutes along the Broad. We can sail there to see if we can catch your husband, if you like?"

Lyn noted Ant's confused looked as she relieved him of the drinks tray and watched both men mourn the loss of their beer as if they were about to have an arm cut off.

"But—"

"But nothing, Ant. Let's get going."

Her tone was not one that anticipated being contradicted.

"Don't worry, your pale ale will still be here when we get back."

Ant took one last peek at his pint.

Hannah started to move towards them.

"No, Hannah. You stay here with Fitch and Annabelle. Don't worry, we'll be back in a jiffy."

"Don't worry, Ant. I'll keep your Fen Bodger safe."

From the look on Fitch's face, Lyn doubted that would be the case.

"Well, it looks peaceful enough," said Lyn as *Fieldsurfer* neared the boathouse.

"Not so sure that's a good sign, Lyn."

Ant brought the vessel to a smooth stop alongside a pair of wide double doors of the old wooden structure that allowed access to and from the Broad. Leaning over the side of the boat, Ant attempted to turn a large, round door handle on one of the doors. It failed to move. He then tried pressing his weight against the heavy doors. Still they stood firm.

"It's a rum do, Lyn. Push us down a bit, will you?"

She retrieved a long wooden pole from the deck and walked to the stern of *Fieldsurfer* and lowered one end into the water until it hit bottom. Using her body weight against the other end, and simultaneously pushing forward, made the wherry move just enough so that it glided without a sound six feet farther down the bank.

Ant secured *Fieldsurfer* against a thick wooden mooring post standing tall from a lush bed of Norfolk reed.

"You go to the right, Lyn. I'll go this way. Shout if you see anything."

The pair jumped from the craft and made their way around opposite sides of the old structure. Coming across a rickety set of doors that punctured an otherwise featureless façade, Ant turned an ancient Bakelite doorknob.

"Wow, what a space."

Ant stood aside allowing Lyn to pass into the cavernous interior. He watched as the loose-fitting timber-wall planks, altered by decades of neglect, allowed pencil-thin shafts of light to penetrate the otherwise darkened interior. Ant placed one foot in front of the other as if passing through a minefield, such was the building's poor state of repair. In the near distance, a gleaming vessel bobbed gently in the water.

It's made from mahogany: must have cost a fortune.

Ant steadied Lyn as she overtook him on the narrow staging. Lyn pointed at the boat.

"Well, if Geoff *is* here, he must be aboard."

Ant stepped onto the craft's immaculate deck.

"Or in the water, Lyn. We'd better check. It's sheltered in here, so he wouldn't have floated out into the Broad."

Ant could tell by her shocked response it wasn't something she wished to contemplate.

Oops, better take the heat out of this.

"I'm only joking, Lyn. I'm certain he's wallowing in some hotel or other with a whiskey until he calms down."

Lyn's frown showed she only half believed him.

"Well, that may be the case, Ant. But I think we should check below all the same. Don't you?"

For someone determined not to think the worst, Ant noted Lyn's lack of hesitation in pulling the deck cover back and launching herself down a set of steep steps.

"Watch your head on the bulkhead... Can you see anything?"

Silence.

"Is anything wrong, Lyn?"

Silence.

"You could say that."

He didn't like the pace or speed of Lyn's response.

Ant descended the steps, turned around, and rubbed his nose.

Dusty in here.

He allowed himself a few seconds to gain his bearings in the craft's dim interior.

Heaven help us.

In front sat a man of around thirty-five, resting backwards against a richly upholstered bench running along one side of the cabin. He looked in a state of total relaxation with his eyes closed and arms at rest on the table in front of him.

Poor man looks as though he's just fallen asleep.

"I'm assuming he's dead?"

Ant turned to Lyn having tried to trace a heartbeat.

"No pulse. And cold."

Ant asked Lyn to double-check.

Her look confirmed the awful truth.

"I assume it's—"

"Hannah's husband? Never met him, but who else could it be, Ant?"

How the hell do we tell his wife?

2

A POLICEMAN CALLS

"Perhaps you think I might thank you for bothering to tell us you'd found a body?"

Nothing if not consistent, Riley.

Ant expected no less from the detective inspector, who fizzed like a firecracker as he scurried into the boathouse, an open mackintosh billowing in his wake.

"Isn't it curious that whenever a corpse turns up, the terrible twosome is to be found lurking. Have a fetish for the recently departed, do you?"

On form today, aren't we.

Both stood aside as the irked policeman strutted along the unstable walkway. A police photographer and scenes-of-crime officer followed.

"And nice to see you again, Detective Inspector. Isn't that so, Lyn."

She smiled.

Riley failed to return the gesture. Ant knew the man had rumbled his sarcastic tone and might try his hand at playing the game.

"I'm surprised to find you here. I thought your sort liked going to the country for the weekend?"

Ant acknowledged the question with a lofty nod.

"Good job I'm already in the country, then, Inspector. Actually, I prefer regattas at Henley, but duty calls, and I am obliged to socialise with the working classes. You understand all about duty, don't you?"

Ant offered a benign smile.

Riley scowled.

Lyn groaned.

"When you two have stopped biting lumps out of each other, you may wish to give your attention to the dead bloke."

She pointed at the boat.

Ant caught her glare, daring him to continue. Her intervention had choked off the torrent of testosterone.

"You are a pompous ass, sometimes, Ant," she whispered.

He looked like a schoolboy about to complain that a dog ate his homework.

Riley shuffled onto the vessel and made for the deck hatch.

"Mind your..." said Ant, placing both hands on his head and crouching as if to avert imminent danger.

Too late.

The inspector let out a cry as his forehead crashed into the top of the cabin doorframe. The force of the blow knocked him backwards against the steep stairs.

Ant felt a tug on his arm as Riley tobogganed out of sight down the stairs and into the boat's interior.

"For goodness' sake, behave yourself. That must have hurt like hell."

A quick glance at Lyn told him to leave it be.

Several minutes passed as camera flashes illuminated

the cabin space, and police officers scoured the deck area. Ant could just make out Riley as he bobbed up and down.

"Watch it, Lyn. Here he comes."

"Well, no suspicious circumstances concerning the gentleman's demise as far as I'm concerned."

Ant feigned a yawn to stop himself laughing as Riley dabbed his head with a handkerchief.

"I'm certain it will comfort you to learn that violent death doesn't follow you around all the time."

Don't smirk at me like that, fool.

Ant turned towards Lyn. He knew she expected him to come out all guns blazing. Instead, he raised an eyebrow at her and nodded.

Lyn accepted the offer.

"How can you be so sure, Inspector?"

Riley checked his forehead again.

"No obvious injuries. No signs of a struggle, and no damage to the boat. In short, a man sat down, closed his eyes and died: end of story."

Ant pointed at the detective's head.

"But your poor bonce. Do you feel as bad as it looks?"

Riley instinctively recoiled as Ant extended a finger towards the eruption.

"Can't be too careful. After all, if a fit young man like that poor chap can cop it minding his own business, then an overweight policeman of a certain age needs to be vigilant when he cracks his skull."

Ant knew that the mention of the injury might encourage Riley to unconsciously touch the savage lump.

He was correct.

Riley winced.

"What my friend means, Inspector, is—"

Oh, do you, thought Ant.

"I know what he means, Miss Blackthorn, and I thank him for his concern."

Blast, he didn't bite.

Ant inwardly gave the detective due recognition for not retaliating as he watched Riley dab his broken skin and inspect his greyish-white handkerchief for blood.

I bet that doesn't half hurt.

"By the way," said Riley, doing up the buttons of his mackintosh. "You forgot to tell me how you two came to be here in the first place."

Ant began to form his response but observed Lyn would beat him to it.

"Luck? That's an odd way of describing a man's death, isn't it? As it happens, we were at a charity BBQ upriver and came across that poor man's wife. To cut a long story short, we offered to come over and see if he was here."

Ant's eyes burned into Riley.

"Turns out he is. Here, I mean, Inspector.

And I bet I know what you're going to say next.

"Did you, indeed, mister, or should I say, *Lord* Stanton? Well, we'll take it from here and get a liaison officer over to Mrs Singleton. This means there will be no need for either of you to trouble yourselves further. Do I make myself clear?"

Ant winked at Lyn.

"The name My Lord will be sufficient, Mr Riley."

Riley scowled but did not engage further as a billowing mackintosh masked the detective's bulk as he exited the boathouse, leaving the remaining officers to complete their work.

"Time to go, I think, Lyn."

Within two minutes, both were on *Fieldsurfer* making ready to cast off.

"You're quiet."

Ant considered Lyn's comment as he watched her stow the wherry's sail and give him the nod to fire up the outboard motor.

"Nothing to say, is there? I hate to admit it, but I think Plod has a point. Geoff looks as though he was just unlucky. Perhaps he had some kind of undiagnosed heart problem. Stuff happens."

Ant chose not to elaborate as he pulled the engine recoil start and pushed the tiller hard to starboard. The wherry turned on a sixpence.

He peered over the edge of the boat to see what Lyn was distracting herself with and glanced at the elongated bodies of several grey mullet skirting the vessel's timber hull.

"But you just don't sit down and die, Ant. At least not someone as young and fit as him?"

He looked up from the water and adjusted the throttle to the permitted maximum of five miles per hour for Stanton Broad.

"Ah, but you can. What about that sudden death syndrome thingy?"

Lyn moved to the centre of *Fieldsurfer* and swung an arm around the vessel's mast.

"You mean sudden arrhythmic death syndrome, Ant. You may be right, but—"

"That's spooky. The acronym spells SADS."

"Rather makes my point, Ant."

One way of finding out.

"I tell you what, Lyn. Why don't you shoot over to Hannah's place? I've got that consultant chappy coming to the Hall with his bright ideas for putting the estate on a sound footing. The police liaison officer is bound to be a woman, so you'll have no problem getting in."

Ant couldn't understand why Lyn started to apologise.

"Goodness. I forgot about your meeting. I'm happy to tag along and keep your parents entertained while you talk turkey.

Ant's look spoke of his appreciation for her concern and offer to shield his parents from what he knew would be a difficult discussion about the Hall's future.

He tried to make light of the situation.

"Bet he recommends some type of theme park. What do you fancy: safari, dinosaur, or a thousand things to make with Norfolk reed?"

Ant raised an open palm to encourage a response.

"You don't fool me, Anthony Stanton."

She can read me like a book.

As Lyn brought the Mini to a stop outside Hannah's house, she spotted a woman talking to Annabelle at the front door.

Must be the liaison officer. Do I go now, or wait for her to leave?

Events resolved themselves. The woman turned and made for her car. Once the Astra had pulled away, Lyn strolled up the brick-weave driveway and rang the doorbell.

After what seemed like an age, the door opened.

"Oh, nice of you to call, Lyn. Hannah will be so pleased to see you. Please, follow me."

Lyn noted Annabelle's reddened eyes.

"I know how horrible it must be for Hannah, but how are you coping?"

Annabelle shrugged her shoulders without making further comment.

Moving down a long, narrow hallway, Lyn followed a

quiet whimper to its source. She watched as Hannah sat crouched in a corner of the spacious lounge, weeping into the folds of a sports jacket.

Got to be Geoff's.

"I'm so sorry, Hannah. I'm sure the police will do everything they can to find out what happened."

Lyn sensed Hannah hadn't heard her. Instead the grieving young woman turned to Annabelle who sat on the arm of a leather sofa looking aimlessly out of the front window.

Poor souls.

"Now, how about a nice cup of tea?"

Neither woman answered. Nevertheless, Lyn made her way to the spacious kitchen, which stretched the full width of the house: the floorspace divided into two by a wide breakfast bar.

As Lyn first filled then flicked on the electric kettle, she couldn't help contrasting the ordinariness of the room with the extraordinary events of the day.

Cruel, but life goes on.

She pushed aside a neat pile of official-looking papers to make room on the worktop. It was as if Geoff had just popped out. Except he wouldn't be coming back.

As Lyn lifted three mugs from the wall cabinet, something fell from the top shelf.

Looks like a business card.

Lyn turned the small rectangular-shaped object over to reveal its owner.

Rufus Dean-Parker
Royal Windsor Yacht Design & Build
Bespoke Conversions

Interesting. I wonder if Geoff was thinking of selling his boat.

Still pondering her discovery, Lyn headed back into the lounge.

"Here we are."

She set a stylish melamine serving tray onto an oak coffee table.

Eventually, Hannah stirred and indicated to Lyn she might like some.

"Milk and sugar? There you are. Now you take a sip of that."

Lyn offered Hannah one of the brightly coloured mugs.

"This is your famous English tea, yes? I bought it in the village when we first moved in."

Lyn nodded and returned Hannah's smile.

Brave girl.

"Tell me about Geoff."

Lyn leant forward, encouraging Hannah to open up about her husband.

Hope this works.

Hannah responded, hesitantly at first. Her smile widened. Lyn knew she was recalling the good times.

"He was so passionate about his work you know. He refused to do business with anyone who didn't share his love for our beautiful world. Geoff worried so much about the damage we are all doing to our planet. His saw it as his mission to help develop clean energy."

Lyn sensed Annabelle moving.

"Hannah is right. He managed to run a successful business and stay true to his beliefs. That is hard to do in business, yes?"

Hannah's smile faded.

"But my husband was stubborn. His uncle and grandfather died young. I told him to see the doctor and check he didn't have the same problem, but he refused. Stupid man."

Lyn knew Hannah didn't mean to sound so angry. It was part of the grieving process.

Not the right time to ask if she knew Geoff was selling their boat.

3

CASTLE AHEAD

A wisp of cloud made lazy progress across the early evening sky like a piece of fluffed cotton as Ant and Lyn strolled around the spacious grounds of Stanton Hall.

"From the look on your face, I assume the business consultant's recommendations didn't impress?"

Lyn linked arms with her best friend by way of offering him support.

"Let's just say I've paid nearly two thousand quid for a bloke in a suit to tell me what I already know."

Ant's tone left little to her imagination.

"Let me guess. A wedding venue, opening the Hall to the public, complete with tearoom, shop stuffed with organic vegetables, and teddy bears wearing Union Jack waistcoats? Also, perhaps, suggesting you stage classical concerts during the summer months?"

Lyn's response served only to increase Ant's agitation.

"Yes, all of it. Plus, would you believe, flooding Water Meadow to reinstate the wetland that apparently existed when Adam was a lad. He says we can then turn it into a blessed bird sanctuary."

Lyn laughed.

"It's not funny."

She tugged on his arm.

"If you don't stop it, your face will stick like that, and then who'd want to visit, except at Halloween?"

His attempt to stifle a fit of giggles failed miserably.

"Actually, Ant, a bird sanctuary sounds rather exciting. And you'd be helping to save the planet."

She watched as he peered at her through narrowed eyes.

"Try telling that to the villagers in Low Road. I doubt they'd like sharing their living rooms with a flock of pink-footed geese when the damn place floods."

Lyn's eyes lit up.

"At least it would save them having to buy a bird for Christmas lunch, Ant. They're expensive, you know."

Who's the gullible one, then.

"Have you lost the plot or what? Water Meadow and Low Road are called as such for good reason. And anyway, they're protected."

Lyn let go of her friend and turned to face him.

"Protected? What, road names?"

Ant's eyes closed as he shook his head.

"The geese, Lyn. The geese... as you well know, Ms Blackthorn."

He tilted his head in mock disdain.

Her eyes flashed.

"Don't you call me—"

Ant lifted an arm and showed Lyn his open palm.

"I apologise, head teacher. Anyway, do you know what they call them?"

Lyn needed no encouragement to drop into teacher mode.

"The singular is goose, the plural, geese."

He laughed.

"No, no. Not the goose... I mean, geese. The business consultant; do concentrate, Lyn."

Unimpressed, she shrugged her shoulders.

"Shall I give you a definition of someone who charges you six hundred smackaroos a day for 'advice'?" He didn't wait for a reply. "Someone who always ends their sentences with 'but on the other hand...'"

Lyn huffed and half turned.

"Serves you right for having more money than sense."

Better move this conversation on.

"Come on, let's get going. I want to reach Stanton Broad in time for the sunset; it looks as though it's going to be a good one.

Lyn gazed at the weakening sun as it continued its inevitable submission to the horizon.

She bumped hips with Ant as they left the grazed pastures of Home Farm and progressed down a gentle slope covered in knee-high great fen-sedge.

Ant responded with a smile and bumped her back.

"Anyway, Lyn, never mind that stupid business consultant. How did you get on with Hannah Singleton?"

Lyn pulled a handful of sedge by giving the plant a sharp tug.

"She was in bits. Thank heavens she's got Annabelle there, that's all I can say. It's bad enough losing your husband, but to be in a strange country as well. That's hard."

Lyn rubbed the swelling seed heads of the sedge between her fingers.

"I get it," replied Ant. His words were spoken with a quiet dignity.

Lyn glanced at her friend, knowing the memory of losing his elder brother could still reduce him to tears.

"She's angry, Ant. It turns out he may have had a congenital heart condition that killed his father and uncle, but he wouldn't get himself checked. Too scared, I guess."

Ant copied Lyn in grabbing a handful of grass.

"Well, well. So I wasn't too far off when I mentioned that syndrome thingy. What if there was something the doctors could have done, and he didn't bother, or as you say, was afraid to find out? No wonder she's angry."

Lyn fell into a reflective mood as she shuffled through a sea of vegetation, grasshoppers springing from the tops of the sedge in response to being disturbed.

"Then again, perhaps he did find out and didn't want to worry Hannah?"

Lyn shook her head.

"I don't think so. Or if he did, he was one cool cookie to keep it from Hannah."

"What do you mean?"

Lyn stopped mid-stride.

"A question—if someone knew for certain they had a serious health condition that, without treatment, might kill them literally in a heartbeat, would they buy a new boat when they already have an almost-new top-of-the-range model?"

Lyn looked towards Ant.

"Could have been on his bucket list, I suppose. Anyway, how do you know he was in the market for a new boat?"

Lyn pulled a small card from her trouser pocket.

"Here, look at this."

Ant read the card, a smile growing as he finished examining its contents.

"Small world. I know Rufus. Geoff must have been loaded, because this guy only sells to the top-drawer crowd who don't have to ask about the price tag."

Lyn sighed.

"I should have known. The aristocrat and a rich boat builder who works for toffs."

Money always sticks together.

"Not sure I would describe some of his clients as the aristocracy, Lyn. Not in the traditional sense, anyway. He works with some dodgy people, which makes their money dodgy. Put it this way. They are most certainly not the sort of people you'd want to fall foul of."

Lyn reclaimed the business card.

"Surprising, that—I mean, given Geoff Singleton's apparent uber-ethical approach to business." She watched Ant frown. "Don't look so confused. It was something Anabelle mentioned."

"Well, there's one way to find out if our young entrepreneur was indeed as pure as the driven snow. I'll give Ruffy a ring to see if we can shoot down to his place tomorrow morning."

Ruffy.

"Ruffy? What is it with you lot that you have to give each other a nickname?"

Ant let out a throaty laugh.

"Mock ye not. It has its advantages as you will see tomorrow."

Lyn didn't appreciate the finger being wagged at her.

"I've wanted to visit Windsor Castle since I was a kid. Don't suppose I'll manage it today, either, judging by the royal standard fluttering above the round tower?"

Lyn marvelled at the immense size of the castle as Ant's beloved Morgan sports car made its way through the narrow streets of Windsor, down the steep incline of High Street and towards the waterfront.

"Have you been in there?"

Ant glanced towards the castle's massive battlements.

"Funny you should ask. I had lunch with some people a couple of years ago. It's a fantastic place. They made a great job of restoring the castle after the fire in 1992. Now it's hard to tell what's twenty years old and which bits date back a thousand years."

Lyn turned to Ant as he changed gear to cope with a tricky corner.

"I meant as a tourist, not a lunch guest of Her Majesty!"

Lyn couldn't believe what he'd just said.

"Strictly speaking, I wasn't. Although I suppose anyone who receives an official invite is, er, the queen's guest. Anyway, can't talk about that. One must never divulge such things, you know."

Lyn hung on his every word, fully expecting him to break the Official Secrets Act.

Ant put a finger to the side of one nostril and gave it a light tap.

"Hush hush and all that."

Lyn bristled, knowing he was playing with her.

Arrogant toerag.

She decided, instead, to ignore anything further he might have to say on the subject. The trouble was, Lyn knew he would expect her, at some point during the day, to demand more detail. And she would give in to temptation.

"Anthony, good to see you. It's been too long, old friend."

Ant had no need to remind himself what a tree of a man

Rufus Dean-Porter was. Six foot five and a dapper dresser with a penchant for Savile Row suits and tailored shirts from Jermyn Street in London. By the time Ant had turned off the purring engine of the Morgan, he realised Rufus was already holding the passenger door open and had extended a firm hand towards Lyn.

Some things never change.

Lyn didn't seem to need further invitation.

"I see you're still paying close attention to the ladies, old chap."

Good Lord, she's blushing?

"Manners maketh the man, Anthony. Isn't that so?"

Ant knew the remark wasn't aimed at him.

"That rather depends on who you ask, Ruffy." He looked towards Lyn and winked.

She is blushing!

"Are you all right, Lyn? You look a bit pink around the gills. I bet it's his driving. Always was mad in his Morgan, which just about sums up Little Lord Fauntleroy."

Didn't take you long to work your charms on Lyn.

Ant's eyes lit up.

"Such a compliment," replied Ant, enjoying every second of Lyn's embarrassment, which also meant he couldn't help noticing her angry eyes burning into him.

"Come on you two. I'll give you a tour of the boatyard before you scratch each other's eyes out."

The yard hugged the Thames shoreline and enjoyed Windsor Castle as its backdrop. The ancient scene looked magnificent in the crisp, sunny morning.

Let's get Ruffy talking.

Rufus explained the site's history, together with the intricacies of high-end, customised boat interiors. It was a story Ant had heard several times through the years. He knew his erstwhile friend would use the opportunity to further impress Lyn.

If her eyes widen any farther, they'll pop their sockets.

"It's a great spot, Rufus. Business good?"

He could see his question irritated Rufus since it forced the charmer to break off his intense gaze holding Lyn captive.

"There's always money at the top end of any market, Anthony. The trouble is getting the blighters to pay their bills. You know the type. The more money they have, the longer they hold on to it!"

Ant laughed.

"So that's the secret. Perhaps I will give it a try it, and see what happens."

"And if they don't pay, now that's when I send 'the boys' round."

Ant knew Rufus was only half joking.

A further ten minutes passed as their tour progressed before Ant turned to business. He watched his guide's body language as he told Rufus about Geoff Singleton's death.

"Now you've got me worried, Ant. He ran an immensely successful equity fund in London, you know. Green technology and all that. I invested a wedge of cash off the back of his sales pitch. He also placed a big contract with me for a custom job on his new boat. Looks like I'm going to get hit twice. And that I don't like at all."

Rufus' demeanour darkened as the implications of Geoff's demise sank in.

But how far will you go to get your money back, Ruffy?

"What did he want you to do?" asked Lyn.

Rufus waved an arm at a gleaming yacht inside the cavernous workshop.

"You know, Lyn. He had a very particular view on how he

wanted the interior fitted out. If you ask me, he had a thing about concealment, bordering on obsession."

Ant's intrigue intensified.

"What do you mean?"

"A concealed cupboard here, a dummy door there, all without any apparent means to opening anything, unless you had the coded remote control, of which there was only to be one. You get used to odd customers in this game, and the richer, the odder, but he took some beating. Then there were the plans for the engine compartment. We were given precise dimensions of the space required, but that was it."

Ant looked into the chasm where the power unit was to be fitted.

"So Geoff intended to fit them himself without telling you their origin? Is that usual?"

Rufus put a hand to his scalp and made as if to scratch his head.

"Good question. No, not normally, not least because of the danger if we, or the customer, gets something wrong and the engine won't fit when we hand the hull back, by which time things have gone rather too far to fix. But Geoff banged on about the power plant being experimental and a trade secret. Some new form of battery was all he would say. Anyway, it was way above my head. He signed off on the dimensions, so as far as I was concerned, that was me off the hook. If they were wrong."

"WHAT DO you make of our Rufus, then?"

Ant's question was tinged with a mix of fascination and jealousy as he accelerated away from Windsor and back toward Stanton Parva.

"He's certainly charming; I'll give you that. But there's something about him that made me uncomfortable, and I can't quite put my finger on it—"

Ant interrupted.

"You mean the flirting?"

He waited for Lyn's response, which was a few seconds in coming.

"No, I, er... Do you know, Ant, it's just—"

"Believe me, Lyn, no one crosses Rufus Dean-Porter without coming off all the worse for it. So, yes, I do know what you mean. Anyway, do you fancy a pear drop?"

The offer was Ant's attempt to lighten the conversation. Ant had seen the gruesome results of Rufus' darker side, which he had no desire to delve into with his best friend.

"Take the bag," added Ant, suddenly in need to scratch an insatiable nose itch.

Catching the sugar-boiled sweet, Lyn made her displeasure clear.

"Get your hand back on the steering wheel before you kill "us both, fool.

4

AN UNSCHEDULED STOP

Ant enjoyed stretching the speed limit of Her Majesty's highways and byways, and for the most part, their journey back to Stanton Parva remained uneventful. That was until he became aware of a particular car in his rear-view mirror.

Any closer, and you'll be in my boot.

"Damn it, where did he come from?"

Unsure of what he was referring to, Lyn looked over her shoulder to see a blue light flashing from the front grill of the vehicle.

"Unmarked police car, serves you right. I've been telling you for the last twenty minutes that you were driving too fast. You'd better hope whichever bobby is in that car is a lover of the aristocracy."

Have they nothing better to do?

"And make sure you keep your temper, Anthony Stanton. No tantrums, do you hear?"

Ant snorted an acknowledgement as he gripped the steering wheel and waited for the inevitable tap on his side window.

Here we go.

Instead of pressing the control to lower the window, he hit the switch next to it. In an instant, an electric motor sprang to life, followed by a solid "click." The Morgan's soft-top roof disengaged, lifted upwards and backwards, then descended to neatly stow itself behind the jump seat.

Ant could feel the bad vibes coming from Lyn. He knew she knew he'd done it on purpose.

He observed that to his immediate right stood a police constable whose uniform was at least one size too small. The man's overturned waistband showing the white lining of his trousers further eroded the dignity of his office as did his need for a shave.

"Trying to be funny, are we, sir?"

The bobby spoke in a low, gravelly voice.

Ant began to form his response, except Lyn beat him to it.

"I'm so sorry, Constable. That was my fault. As you can see, the two button thingies are so close together. My friend intended to let the window down, and I inadvertently nudged him, making his hand slip."

Ant continued to look straight ahead, working hard to keep a straight face.

Nice one, Lyn.

The policeman spent a few seconds pushing the tail of his shirt back into his trousers before responding. Satisfied no further mechanical surprises awaited, the burly copper leant forward, forcing Ant to crane his neck to make eye contact with the bobby.

"I see. Is that the case, sir?"

Instead of responding, he watched the towering policeman stare rather too long at Lyn for his liking.

"I'll let it pass on this occasion—"

Right. That's it.

Unable to help himself, Ant bit.

"Why, exactly, have you pulled me over, Officer?"

The policeman stiffened.

"I was just coming to that, sir."

Ant knew the officer's overemphasis of the word "sir" meant he was rattled.

Lyn will make me pay for that.

He didn't have to wait long.

Ant felt a sharp dig into his left side and winced as her blow landed.

"Something wrong, sir?"

Ant took a deep breath as he glimpsed Lyn's index finger pointing at his aching ribs. He understood her warning.

"Not at all, Officer. Just curious, that's all."

The policeman smirked.

"Just a routine traffic stop, sir. That's all. We've had reports of drunk drivers on this stretch of road. You haven't had a drink today, have you, sir?"

Not wishing for a further poke in the ribs, Ant suppressed his natural urge to aggravate the policeman.

"Not at all, Officer. Not one drop has passed our lips."

The policeman leant farther into the car, sniffing the air in an exaggerated manner, ending up inches from Ant's right cheek.

Keep your distance, pal.

He was within seconds of pushing the copper away for invading his personal space when the man relented.

The huge copper stepped away from the car, moving his attention from Lyn to glare at Ant.

"Well, I can't smell alcohol on your breath, sir, so on this occasion we will let the matter drop."

Strange he's not following police procedure by breathalysing me if he suspected I'd been drinking?

"Will that be all, Officer?"

Ant almost spat the words through clenched teeth.

Lyn flashed her index finger again. Ant glared at his friend. She blinked first and, instead, gave the policeman a broad smile.

What are you up to?

Unable to control his base instincts, the constable returned her smile as if she'd just accepted an offer of dinner for two.

"Just one last thing, sir. May I ask the reason for your visit to Windsor, today?"

He spoke without taking his eyes off Lyn.

Keep it up, girl.

Lyn succeeded in meeting her friend's unspoken challenge.

Meanwhile, Ant gripped the steering wheel with such force that his knuckles began to turn white.

This is Riley's doing. He's put us under surveillance.

"They do have some wonderful boats for sale down there, don't they, sir?"

That does it.

Ant fumed as he realised something more serious than a routine traffic stop was occurring.

He gave the official a defiant glare.

"We didn't say anything about Windsor or boats."

The policeman stepped forward so that he once again towered over Ant.

"No, you didn't, did you, sir?"

Ant took note that the man, whoever he was, spoke with a chill that would shame packed ice.

"Well, that will be all, and I apologise if I have delayed

you, sir. I know how precious time is when you're on leave, especially sick leave."

The policeman took two steps backwards, smirked, then gestured for Ant to continue his journey.

Ant was aware that his theory about Riley risked turning into a self-fulfilling prophecy as he fumed at the policeman's knowledge of their movements, and his personal circumstances.

Allowing his emotions to override caution, Ant pressed his right foot to the floor. The sports car responded immediately.

For several minutes he tore up the tarmac on the narrow, twisting country roads, lost in a world of his own.

"Time to slow down, cowboy."

Ant failed to respond. Instead, his eyes remained in a trance-like state as his grip on the steering wheel tightened still further.

Suddenly he felt Lyn's touch over his clenched left hand. Bodily contact did the trick and broke his anger.

"Cup of tea and a cake, don't you think?"

Ant turned to Lyn, offered the beginnings of a smile, and eased his foot off the accelerator.

You know how to handle me. I'll give you that.

"TWO AFTERNOON TEAS," said the young waiter as he brought a serving trolley to a stop by the side of a small square table.

"Yes, that's us. Thank you so much," replied Lyn.

Ant surveyed the elegant cake stand freshly loaded with a selection of sandwiches, cakes, and cream scones.

Leaving a pot of tea for two, the server withdrew, leaving Ant and Lyn to relax as they looked over Sheldon Broad from the spacious conservatory of The Water's Edge tearooms.

"It's all right for some."

Ant's comment summed up his view of the wildlife scurrying about on the mill's pond-like surface of the water stretching into the distance.

"Calmed down, yet?"

Ant frowned. As far as he was concerned, the moment had passed, and he was now perfectly calm.

"You know what the doctor said, Ant. Your PTSD is not going to go away without treatment."

Ant didn't acknowledge Lyn's comment or break eye contact with the water. The seconds passed as a silence descended.

Suppose I'd better say something.

"For the most part, I don't think about it. Then something sets it off and..."

Lyn didn't respond, other than to hold up the plate she'd filled for him. He looked at her, smiled, and took his food.

I know you get me.

"Anyway, what do you think about our mysterious bobby. And what was that stuff about Windsor?"

He was thankful she'd let his illness drop, at least for now.

Ant bit into a cucumber sandwich, which delayed his response by all of the five seconds it took to demolish the tiny snack.

"Odd might be one way to describe it. Riley has to be behind us being stopped. The question is why? What's he up to?"

Eyeing the selection of sandwiches on his plate, Ant selected the fresh salmon.

"So you're changing your mind about Geoff's death?"

Ant took a last lingering look at his sandwich before devouring it in one go.

"Let's put it this way, Riley wouldn't authorise one of his goons to tail us unless he thinks Geoff's death is suspicious. And if the force is interested in Geoff's demise, I suppose I should be too, don't you think?"

He could see that his reply met with Lyn's approval.

"Well, that took you long enough. So where do we go from here?"

Ant considered his options.

"Let's talk about it over dinner—my treat."

Lyn sighed as she looked at her mobile to check the time.

"Sorry. I've got a staff meeting tomorrow that I need to prepare for and a stack of marking to do. Can we give it a miss?"

Ant feigned disappointment as he grabbed the last piece of sponge cake from the stand.

"In that case, I'd better eat this lot. Tell you what. I'll do a bit of digging by giving Riley a poke tomorrow morning."

Lyn frowned and wagged an index finger.

"Make sure you behave yourself, young man, or it'll be the legal type of detention you'll be dealing with, not one of my school stay behinds."

Ant let out a roar that caused heads to turn.

"Yes, head teacher. Message understood."

Lyn nodded as if confirming the threat to one of her young pupils.

"And I'll call on Hannah after school to see how she's getting on."

5

MONDAY BLUES

Ant almost convinced himself that time had stood still as he gazed at a photo on the wall of the police station dating back over a hundred years compared to the reality of the building today.

As he leant on an old-fashioned oak countertop waiting to be attended to, he imagined the number of people, guilty and innocent, that had passed through the space he now stood over, the previous fifteen decades or so.

"Good morning, sir. How may I help you today?"

Ant awoke from his distraction as two huge hands gripped the opposite edge of the counter. He recognised their owner as Sergeant Fredrick Cummins who, as far as Ant knew, had been a policeman from the beginning of time and who had collared him more than once for making mischief as a young lad.

"Might I have a word with Detective Inspector Riley?"

Ant always felt as though he'd done something wrong and was about to be arrested when in the presence of a policeman.

Guess they must be trained to look at you like that.

Before the policeman could answer, the desk telephone rang. Ant waited patiently as the sergeant became increasingly exasperated with his caller.

"I can absolutely assure you, sir, there is no need to report running over a cat to the police. A dog, yes. A cat, no."

Several seconds passed while the policeman listened to the caller again.

"It is of no concern to the police that this Mrs Tennant you mention has threatened you with a citizen's arrest. You have committed no crime. Ruined the cat's day, yes, but executed a crime, no. You see, in the eyes of the law, a cat has no legal owner. The fact this lady bought it a toy mouse and fed the animal best-quality chicken each day counts for nothing as far as we are concerned. Will that be all, sir?"

The desk sergeant didn't wait for an answer. Instead, he replaced the handset and made a quick note of the call in the duty log.

"Now what did you say you wanted to report. It's not another cat, is it?"

Ant held his tongue, having decided any further mention of felines would be of little help to his cause.

"I didn't... want to report running over a cat, I mean."

The policeman looked confused.

"Detective Inspector Riley. Is he in?" repeated Ant.

Eventually, the penny dropped.

"That rather depends on why you want to see him, sir. He's a very busy man as I am sure you will understand."

Ant's patience had its limits.

"For goodness' sake, Fred. Is he in, or isn't he? What's up with you today?"

He watched Sergeant Cummins retrieve a pack of

headache tablets from his breast pocket, squeeze two capsules from the blister pack, and try swallowing them without liquid, which caused the policeman to pull an anguished face when they got stuck.

"That bad," said Ant as he raced the few feet to a water fountain and dispensed just enough water into a flimsy plastic cup to help Fred get his medication down.

Fred nodded his thanks and almost choked on the mixture of liquid and tablets before letting out a sigh of relief.

"Better?"

Fred nodded his head while rubbing two fingers in a circular motion to massage the pain away.

"It's him in there. In a stinking mood, he is."

Fred pointed half-heartedly at a door behind Ant.

"Perhaps the wife had a go at him for leaving his toe clippings on the floor again—he does it here as well, you know. Horrible habit. Anyway, he's been shouting at everyone since he arrived. Drives me mad, he does."

Ant smiled.

"I'm not going to let you see him if you're going to make him worse, Lord Stanton or not."

"Me?"

Ant pointed a finger at himself and offered the stressed policeman a hurt look.

"Yes, you. I know what you're like with him, so behave, understand? My head can't put up with much more today."

"Behave with who?"

Fred stiffened, immediately recognising the voice.

"This gentleman has asked to see you, sir."

The desk sergeant gave no further information. Riley started to extend his hand before quickly retracting the offer as Ant turned to face him.

"Oh, it's you."

Ant responded with a broad smile.

"And a very good morning to you, Detective Inspector. Might I have a word? I know you will be dreadfully busy, but..."

Riley scowled.

Ant's smile broadened.

"Get me a coffee, Sergeant. And you, follow me."

Both men did as they were ordered with Fred making for the staff kitchen and Ant following the detective into a small, poorly lit, windowless office.

As the detective reached the halfway point between standing and taking his seat, Ant pounced.

"Why are you having me followed?"

Ant could tell he'd unsettled him as the flummoxed policeman hovered for a few seconds before settling his ample backside into the padded leather seat of his ancient, civil service, standard-issue chair.

"What are you talking about, man?"

Now let's see what happens.

Riley fidgeted with a pile of papers and sought out his favourite fountain pen for the want of something to do.

Ant sat opposite Riley and leant into the table, closing the distance between them deliberately, before recounting events from the previous day.

Riley's facial expression changed from irritation to outright confusion.

He's a good actor; I'll give him that.

"Tall, overweight officer? Roadside stop? Have you gone mad?" Believe me, I'd have been told if one of my officers had stopped the noble Lord Stanton."

Riley's smile confirmed to Ant that the detective relished the thought of him being subjected to public indignity.

"Sounds to me like you've fallen victim to someone impersonating a police officer. We've had several such reports recently."

Ant hesitated, unsure how to respond.

Telling the truth or winding me up? One way to find out.

"A new strategy to increase the police's presence, is it? You know, if you can't put your own out, get some bloke in fancy dress to do the job for you?"

Ant counted on his words stinging Riley. They did.

"I can assure you—"

Ant pulled his usual trick of cutting the detective off in mid-sentence.

"Then how did he know about me being in Windsor? And my military background?"

Ant spoke harshly. He was in no mood to be fobbed off.

Riley stood up and paced around his dingy office.

"I have absolutely no idea, but it's not as if you are exactly anonymous in these parts, is it?"

Touched a nerve there all right.

"Let me get this straight, Detective Inspector. You're saying Geoffrey Singleton's death and me being warned off by the police aren't linked?"

Riley pulled a well-worn handkerchief from a side pocket and blew his nose into the off-white material.

"Warned off? Warned off from what? Mr Singleton died from natural causes, and the post-mortem tomorrow will confirm as much. That is, unless you have information to the contrary. Remember, Lord Stanton, I have warned you before about interfering in police work and withholding evidence. I will not hesitate to arrest you if I have the slightest evidence this is the case."

Need to be careful here.

Before Riley could interrogate Ant further, the detective's phone rang.

"Of course, sir, right away."

Riley gave no explanation as he made for the door. As he did so, the handle moved downward hitting Riley across the knuckles.

"I'm sorry, sir," said Fred while holding the detective's mug of coffee in his free hand. His smirk was unmistakable as Riley inspected the flesh covering his knuckles for damage.

"Get out of my way, man, and show this person out."

Result!

"You said you wouldn't upset him."

"I suspect the summons to his superior's office is rather more to blame for his mood than my visit... although I admit, it might be a close-run thing."

Both men laughed.

"Been doing any scrumping lately, young Stanton?"

Ant was happy to recall old times.

"I lost count how many times you walloped me across the head and sent me on my way, Fred. But thanks for never telling my parents!"

Lyn placed a comforting arm around Hannah as they sat together on a large crimson leather sofa.

"I thought you could do with a bit of company. How are you?"

Hannah repeated how gentle Geoff was and that the success of their business meant they had no money worries.

"It's not fair. We had only just got married."

Lyn encouraged Hannah to talk before eventually managing to swing the conversation around to Geoff's boat.

"So you're saying he intended to sell it?"

"Yes, he had a new one on order." Lyn offered Hannah a tissue as she mopped tears from her cheek. "He went to the boathouse to finish off some little jobs on the yacht. Varnishing the wood, I think. I hated the smell of that stuff. It was okay for him; he had no sense of smell. Geoff loved, how you say, doing the DIY?"

Lyn nodded and offered a friendly smile.

"Yes, Hannah, that's what we call it."

"But why do you ask me this?"

Better watch how far and fast I go now.

"Oh, you know. Small village, people gossip."

Hannah frowned.

"Gossip? What is gossip?"

Lyn attempted to explain.

"Er, let me see. Well, people who talk to each other about a new bit of news. One tells another, and they tell—"

"Oh, yes. I understand. We call it plotka."

Lyn's eyes lit up.

"Well, what do you know. I've learned a little Polish today. Thank you, Hannah."

The women passed the next few minutes talking about daily life in a small village. Detecting she'd succeeded in helping Hannah relax, Lyn took her opportunity and pressed on.

"And the police. Have you heard from them?"

Lyn tried not to sound too inquisitive.

"Ah, how do you say? Er... liaison officer, yes, I have it. That lady came to the house, how you say... earlier."

Hannah broke down.

"It's okay. You cry all you want."

"No, you don't understand. They are going to cut him up tomorrow. Too horrible. His heart stopped working. Why do they have to do this?"

Lyn worked hard to keep her own emotions in check.

"Do you mean a post-mortem?"

Hannah nodded.

"Please tell them to stop. I will not let them."

6

BODY OF EVIDENCE

"Gone, what do you mean, it's gone?"

Ant knew who was complaining as he walked down a poorly lit corridor that led to the mortuary.

He's having a good day—not.

Seconds later, Ant gingerly opened one of two wide doors giving access to the cold, featureless space. It was just enough to catch a whiff of formaldehyde.

I hate that stuff.

His attention was drawn to two figures standing on opposite sides of a white ceramic autopsy slab.

Ant watched on in amusement as Detective Inspector Riley fumed as he gazed upon the surface on which Geoff Singleton's corpse should have lain.

A nervous-looking man in a white laboratory coat looked forlornly at the slab then at Riley. Ant assumed the man didn't know quite what to say.

The less you say, the better you'll come out of this.

Opening the door a touch wider so he could follow the action but still not be noticed, Ant's eyes traced Riley's progress as he prowled around the spacious room, faced with Victorian, white-glazed tiles, before coming to a halt in front of a bank of square metal doors stacked in pairs from floor to ceiling.

"Open them, every last one. He must be here somewhere."

Ant stifled a giggle as he contrasted the pale pallor and slim build of the young lab assistant with Riley's big frame and rapidly reddening cheeks.

The mortuary assistant sprang into action not wishing to incur further wrath from the scowling policeman. As he opened each door, a pair of upturned feet presented themselves, each with a paper tag attached to a big toe.

"Slide each one out. I want to see faces."

Obeying, the technician pulled a handle and walked backwards allowing the contents to extend from the flat surface like a stream of bunting pulled from a conjurer's hat.

Riley pulled back a white linen sheet from each owner's head and carefully inspected the facial features. His mood darkened as he rejected each body in turn.

Ant inwardly agreed with the young man's tactic of taking a step back and towards the exit doors each time Riley let loose a string of invective.

As the policeman looked up to check the whereabouts of the hapless man, Ant pulled his head back so he wouldn't be seen.

"Not so fast, Batman," shouted Riley as he caught the technician's attempted escape. "Please tell me how you managed to lose a dead man? I presume you checked that he was, in fact, dead and that he's not just nipped out for a coffee?"

Very good, Inspector. Not at all bad for you.

An uneasy standoff followed. Eventually, the young man attempted an explanation.

"We were just about to start the post-mortem when the fire alarm went off. We evacuated the building like we're supposed to, and when we came back, it, I mean he, had gone."

Ant had to put a fist into his mouth to stop himself laughing. It got so bad that, as he leant back against the painted wall of the corridor, he resorted to pinching an earlobe with his free hand, so that the pain might distract him from laughing out loud and being discovered.

Achieving his aim, he felt confident enough to continue peeking into the room, only to see the technician shrugging his shoulders.

No use looking for sympathy from that fool, mate.

Riley referenced a fire alarm in the far corner then at the wide entrance doors.

His eyes narrowed.

For once Riley was too quick for Ant.

"I might have known. Is there nowhere you don't manage to show up where you're not wanted?"

After struggling for a nanosecond to understand Riley's poor use of grammar, Ant threw open the door and ambled in with the air of a man out for a stroll in the morning sun.

"Good day to you, Detective Inspector. I was just in the area and—"

"In the area? So you have a fetish for dead bodies? Oh, wait a minute, you do, don't you?"

Second reasonable joke in five minutes. You're on fire today.

Ant smiled, which irritated Riley all the more, then looked at the hapless technician who seemed to be having trouble taking matters in.

"Don't worry about me, young man, I'm—"

"Yes, I know who you are, Lord—"

"Oh, let's not start all that aristocracy stuff again.

Enough. I want to know where my body is. As for you, Stanton. Get yourself out of my sight before I have you arrested."

Ant took faux offence at Riley's tone.

"Me? I didn't steal your body. A bit careless if you ask me, but—"

Ant's provocation had its desired effect.

"But nothing. I neither want nor need your contribution in this matter. Now you have a choice: leave and go back to fishing, or whatever you people do, or you can spend the day in one of my cells. Your choice."

Ant raised an eyebrow at the rattled policeman, knowing it would do the man's humour no good at all.

"Sorry to disappoint you, Inspector. I don't possess a rod or any other implement for catching living creatures. Except for a camera, of course. As for your kind offer of accommodation for the day, perhaps I'll give it a miss on this occasion. I have things to do, you know, supervising the polishing of the family silver and so forth..."

Not getting rid of me that easily, thought Ant as he made for the doors, allowed them to swing shut and waited a few seconds before opening one by the tiniest amount.

He could just about see Riley shaking his head as he returned his attention to the laboratory technician.

"And did whoever took him thoughtfully return the trolley they carted him out in?"

Riley pointed to a metal gurney that had seen better days.

With the restricted view Ant now had, he could just make out the technician turning sideways to follow Riley's index finger.

"We have two. You know, for busy shifts."

"Busy shifts? You make the place sound like *Holby City* on steroids."

Third joke of the morning, Riley. I'm impressed.

The assistant attempted to explain the ward procedures for moving deceased patients from the hospital ward. Ant could see Riley was having none of it.

"Stop. I am not interested in the finer points and progress of rigor mortis or the sensibilities of adjacent live patients. Get me the CCTV so I can watch our body snatchers go about their business."

The technician spotted Ant, froze, and looked back towards the detective without saying a word.

Good lad.

"Now will do," shouted Riley.

"There is none. Pictures I mean."

Ant watched as the young man closed his eyes as if half expecting the detective to land a blow.

"They're upgrading the system. We got an email about it the other day from the big bosses."

Ant readied himself to intervene as he observed Riley lift his right hand and clench his fist. Instead, the detective punched the mortuary slab then winced in pain.

Serves you right, fool.

"You couldn't make it up," whispered the detective inspector as he turned, cradling his injured fist into his ample stomach.

Ant realised Riley was heading in his direction. He raced to the left and hid behind a large stainless-steel trolley piled high with crisp, white, bed linen. It worked, as Riley launched himself in the opposite direction.

After a few seconds, Ant checked that the coast was clear before ambling back into the mortuary.

He smiled. The young man, reassured, smiled back.

"He doesn't half shout, does he?"

Ant grinned all the more.

"He certainly does, but well done, fella. You handled him well. I don't suppose you're used to strangers coming in here —apart from the cold ones on a trolley, of course. And they don't answer back or shout at you, do they?"

He could see his banter was having the desired effect as the young man broadened his smile, held an empty mug up, and pointed at the kettle.

"Thank you, but no."

The technician returned the mug to the sink drainer.

"I suppose that's why I like working down here. You know, for all the shouting and bad stuff people get up to, there's one thing for certain. We will all end up in one of those."

Ant nodded as the young man pointed at the bank of steel doors holding their current crop of corpses.

A wise head on young shoulders.

"And on that bombshell, I'll leave you to it. Again, well done my friend."

Ant offered the technician a "thumbs-up" sign as he exited the chilled room.

Got to catch up with Riley to see what he's about.

A few seconds later, Ant glimpsed the detective as he made his way from the building into a Victorian-walled courtyard. He was shouting into his mobile phone.

"I want this area swept and all road junctions put under covert surveillance."

Ant thought Riley would burst as he grew increasingly agitated.

Guess the news isn't good.

"A burger van, hearse, motorbike with a sidecar. In fact, a horse and cart, for all I care. In fact, anything capable of moving and concealing a corpse is to be checked. Do I make myself clear?"

"What's so funny?" asked Lyn as she entered Hammond's Bakery for her usual Tuesday lunchtime fix of fresh iced buns as a shared treat with her secretary, Tina.

"You haven't heard?"

Geraldine, the shop manager who Lyn knew had a well-earned reputation for having a macabre sense of humour, looked delighted by Lyn's ignorance.

"Them lot up there have lost someone. A body, would you believe? I mean, how do you do that?"

Geraldine cocked her head in the approximate direction of the hospital.

Lyn watched as the manager broke into another fit of laughter.

"I suppose that accounts for all those police sirens I heard. It caused havoc at school. The children wouldn't settle and wanted to know what was going on."

Lyn's question set the other shop assistants into a collective fit of the giggles.

"The bobbies are going bonkers. Checking everywhere, they are."

How odd, thought Lyn.

"Came in here about half an hour ago, they did. Asked if we'd seen anything suspicious."

The shop descended into chaos with two customers almost crying into paper tissues as group hysteria took hold.

"I told the young constable that a tired-looking bloke, who seemed a bit anaemic, got off a trolley and came in asking for a Cornish pasty. Would you believe, the lad asked if I could describe him before he cottoned on he was having his leg pulled."

Lyn shed tears of laughter as she watched Geraldine

almost bent double and holding her stomach as she delivered the punchline.

"Then we told the young bobby that if the bloke wasn't dead before he came in, he would be after eating anything we baked."

It was difficult for Lyn to know where to look. At the sight of Geraldine gasping for air, or the counter staff running for the shop restroom to deal with overexcited bladders.

Lyn worked hard with those who remained in the shopfront by not looking at each other for fear of setting themselves off again. She was thankful that after several seconds of disciplined silence, order replaced chaos.

"But that poor Polish lady. What must she be going through?"

Lyn's ears pricked up. She hadn't expected Geraldine to make such a solemn remark after their collective joviality.

"Polish lady?"

And how does she know about Hannah?

"My Ernie is a porter at the hospital. He rang me this morning to tell me what happened. All hell is breaking loose he says."

Lyn held her surprise in check. She knew any overreaction would be around the village within hours as the gossip mill churned at full speed.

"How awful," replied Lyn as she collected the paper bag containing her iced buns from the Formica counter. "Talking about your Ernie, how long have you two been engaged now?"

The shop erupted into laughter again as they anticipated Geraldine's answer.

"Twenty-two years April gone. That's longer that I would have got for murder."

"Sorry, I'm a bit behind today," said Fitch as Lyn walked onto the garage forecourt to collect her Mini Clubman.

"Not to worry, it happens to the best of us," she replied while glancing at a car bumper lying in two pieces on the yard floor.

"That looks expensive. I'm glad it wasn't my car."

Fitch smiled as he swept the plastic debris to one side with the instep of his foot.

"And Irene Chapman wasn't best pleased either. It turns out some maniac clipped her car early Saturday morning on that nasty bend near the boathouse. They didn't even stop, so that's her insurance no-claims discount up the swanny."

Lyn glanced across to a sorry-looking Nissan Micra, minus a front bumper and with a nasty dent in a wing panel.

"Ouch. I hate people who don't stop after an accident. I bet they didn't have car insurance."

"Happened to me once," replied Fitch. "Cost me a packet to fix—and that was just the parts."

Lyn nodded in sympathy.

"Anyway, I've got to get a move on. I spent too long in Hammond's bakery gossiping about missing bodies. If I don't get back to school pronto, Tina won't get her iced buns, and believe me, that's not a pretty sight."

"It's a rum do though, Lyn. How does a body just disappear into thin air: creepy or what?"

Lyn shrugged her shoulders.

"The thing is, I spent some time with Hannah yesterday. She was adamant in not wanting Geoff's body touched."

Fitch frowned.

"Well, you can't blame her for that, can you, Lyn?"

The conversation was interrupted by the wailing of yet another police car speeding through the village.

"They've been at that all morning," added Fitch.

"Same at school. A real nuisance. But this Hannah thing. You don't think she could have arranged for someone to nab the body, do you? You know, to stop the autopsy taking place?"

Fitch shook his head.

"Can't see it myself. But then I've never been in that position. What I do know is that grief can make some people do crazy stuff."

Lyn nodded then glimpsed the lit screen on her mobile.

"Got to go, or I really will be in Tina's bad books."

In seconds, Lyn was out the gates and striding along the cobbled path back towards Stanton Parva Primary.

"The Mini. It will be ready by five."

Lyn acknowledged Fitch's shout by lifting an arm and waving her hand without looking back. She was too busy concentrating on another matter.

He looks a bit odd.

She had noticed a man in dishevelled clothing and shoes with holes in their toes, shuffling towards her. As he neared, Lyn attempted to catch sight of his face. With his coat collar up and head lowered, Lyn could only see what looked like a faded scar on his right cheek.

The man brushed passed her without missing a step, knocking Lyn off balance.

Wouldn't like to meet him on a dark night.

7

ODD MAN OUT

The outer office of Lyn's room looked like a battlefield clearing station as Ant pushed aside the half-glazed door and stepped inside.

It was several seconds before Tina noticed his presence as she dealt with 3 seven-year-olds in various states of distress.

"Oh, it's you. Don't mind the noise, they'll settle down when I've dished out the stickers for being brave little soldiers."

"What on earth's been going on here?"

Tina gazed up at Ant from the crouched position in front of one of the sobbing boys.

"This one is Timmy Weston. None the worse for wear from an overzealous football tackle. That lad is Billy Lightfoot, a name not associated with his tendency to trip over the smallest of obstacles. And finally, we have young Master Hayman. He's Timmy's avowed enemy in all things football."

Ant noticed that the latter seemed the braver of the three, almost as if he were gloating at Timmy's tears and that his own injured shin had not reduced *him* to a babbling wreck.

"There you are." The voice belonged to Lyn as she breezed into Tina's casualty clearing station.

"Come in, come in. I thought I'd lost you," she said as she gave each of the boys a sympathetic look before quickly moving on to her own office and leaving Tina to tend the injured.

Ant gave the secretary a weary look in acknowledgement of Lyn's "can do" mood and nodded when Tina rolled her eyes.

"She had two cups of coffee an hour ago and hasn't come down yet," replied Tina. "You go in. I think we'll go for green tea when I've discharged the troops, or there will be no handling madam this afternoon."

Ant required no encouragement to escape the organised chaos around him.

"Where have you been? I've been trying to get hold of you since yesterday," asked Lyn as she simultaneously read a missive from the Department for Education.

When you're ready, girl.

Ant waited as it took Lyn a good forty-five seconds to realise he hadn't answered. He watched as she looked up from the briefing paper.

"Ah, got your attention, then, have I? It's no use you blinking at me like one of your pupils who doesn't want to hear he's in trouble."

"I *was* listening."

A gesture of the head and eye contact on the document did the trick. Lyn took the hint and put the briefing note down, making sure one long side rested parallel to the desk edge.

"Listening to what? I didn't say anything."

That tore it.

"Listen, smarty pants, I've got Mr and Mrs Sandown in half an hour to bend my ear about their son—again, so I'm not in the mood for your nonsense. Now, where were you yesterday?"

Ant felt as if he were back in Riley's office, except Lyn was scarier.

"Fair play, old girl. To tell you the truth... Ouch!"

Ant's explanation was interrupted by a pencil catching him square on the forehead, point first.

"How many times have I told you not to call me that?"

This is fun.

"Okay, sorry." Ant checked to see if the graphite was still attached to the end of the pencil or embedded in his flesh.

"I was only joking, Lynda."

Light the blue touch paper and stand back.

Ant watched as Lyn began to flush knowing his apology was half hearted, and the use of her full first name was a calculated jibe to wind her up even more.

Tin hats on.

"Listen, Lord Stanton, or whatever you are calling yourself today, either behave or I'll set those three little terrors in Tina's office on you. Now are you going to answer my question?"

The threat was enough for Ant to capitulate. He held his hands above his head as Lyn continued her interrogation without giving him the opportunity to respond.

"When I rang your dad to see if he knew where you were, he said you'd taken Mr Churchill's dog for a walk. What in heaven's name did he mean?"

Lyn's glare meant Ant had no option but to come clean. After a few seconds spent gathering his thoughts, he slouched back into his chair and looked at the deep-brown material of the carpet.

"Winston Churchill battled depression all his life." He watched Lyn's expression change. The penny had dropped. "It's Dad's way of explaining how I deal with my PTSD. As I've told you before, anything can set the damn thing off. As it happens, yesterday I caught a news item about the Middle East. Another time it wouldn't have affected me. Yesterday it did. I don't know why, but something went 'ding' in my head, and I broke out in a cold sweat."

Ant's eyes followed Lyn as she got up, walked around the desk and perched herself on a corner beside his chair and placed an arm around his shoulders.

"You took off, then?"

"Yes, I did. Not proud of myself but…"

His voice tailed off as Lyn stroked his hair. He could feel himself relaxing in the company and touch of someone he trusted without question.

"Anyway, the dog is back in its kennel so that's that." He gently moved Lyn's hand from his scalp and straightened his back into the chair.

"For now, anyway, Ant. For now. Anyway, how did you get on with Riley yesterday?"

He didn't get a chance to explain before a movement of the door handle and the sight of Tina's head popping through the opening told Ant the Sandowns had arrived. He sensed the change of mood and made to leave.

"I think I'll have a walk around the village. Not done that for ages. Catch up at yours tonight?"

Lyn nodded as she fumbled on her desk for the demanding parents' latest letter of complaint.

"Er, yes," replied Lyn as she looked in panic at Tina.

"Around seven thirty, and the Chinese takeaway is on you. I'll have the usual."

"It's here," said Tina in a quiet, reassuring voice.

"Haven't seen you in here for ages," said David Ingram as Ant stepped over the threshold of the family-run newsagent.

"You do too good a job of delivering the papers. She never misses a day, does she? But that means there's no need to call in except when I fancy some of your scrumptious sweets, so here I am." Ant's saliva glands worked overtime as he surveyed a wall of temptation in what seemed like a hundred old-fashioned glass candy jars.

The newsagent smiled.

"Good to hear. I'll tell young Sophie what you said. Now what can I tempt you with?"

David stood aside allowing Ant an uninterrupted view of the confectionary on offer. Suddenly his face lit up like a Christmas tree.

"I haven't seen those since I was at school. We used to call in here every day, you know."

David pointed to a glass jar of aniseed balls.

"Yep, that's them." Ant's eyes followed David's movement as he stretched to retrieve the jar from a high shelf, place it on the counter, unscrew the large plastic lid, and begin to weigh its contents on a set of scales.

"We used to ask for two ounces when I was a lad. Not sure what that is in grams or whatever they are now." Ant watched each red spherical treat fall from the stainless-steel scoop and into the stainless-steel weighing bowl.

The newsagent laughed.

"I know what you mean, Ant. Ounces sound so much better, don't they? Keep to tradition, I say."

Once David finished dispensing the confectionary into its paper bag, Ant grabbed it and plunged one of the sweets into his mouth.

"Anybody would think I've just given you a pot of gold."

Ant sucked on the hard-boiled sweet and savoured the aniseed's strong flavour.

"You've no idea, Dave."

The smile on his face said it all.

As Ant thanked the shopkeeper and turned to leave, he spotted the latest edition of *Boating World*.

"Can I take one instead of you delivering it?"

David grabbed the paper delivery book from under the counter.

"No problem. Just let me mark it in here, so you don't get another copy. That reminds me. An odd-looking chap asked if I knew where the rich Englishman with the boat lived. I didn't let on because he looked a bit shifty. Mind you, I suppose that was good enough reason to have told him where you lived."

The shopkeeper laughed.

"What, because he was odd, or I'm supposed to be the rich kid?" replied Ant joining in the light-hearted banter. "If you see him again, tell him I'm broke and have left the country for a Buddhist retreat."

Ant left David still laughing as he headed up High Street.

AFTER TWENTY MINUTES of navigating the narrow back streets of the village centre, Ant took a breather by resting against one of the village's prized Victorian, red-pillar boxes. It was just tall enough for him to rest an arm on top to support himself while he read an article from his magazine about a new form of battery technology for boats predicted to take the market by storm within the year.

Soaking in the warm afternoon sun, he noticed a familiar figure coming out of a long-closed Methodist chapel across the road. It was Annabelle.

"It's a small world; what are you up to?" said Ant as she crossed the narrow lane.

"I love your quaint villages and their beautiful buildings."

Ant followed Annabelle's outstretched arm as she waved it around to reinforce her point. "I am interested in buying this old church. I want to convert it into a nice home. The agent was kind enough to let me in. You English are always so polite."

In your dreams, lady.

"I hope you don't mind me asking, but for someone on the hunt for a property, you look a bit glum."

Ant could see he had confused her.

"What is 'glum'?"

He smiled.

"Sorry, with your English being so good, I forgot. It means looking sad."

Oops, she looks even worse now.

"Yes, I see. To be honest, I am worried about Hannah."

Ant's smile vanished as it dawned it was, perhaps, still too early for levity.

"Worried? What's the problem?"

Annabelle slouched against the pillar box, her eyes glazed with emerging tears.

"I have seen a man from Hannah's past. He is trouble. How do you say—he has a terrible temper—very jealous."

The tears began to flow. Ant knew he wasn't the most tactful of individuals at the best of times. Now he hadn't a clue what to do other than to keep asking questions.

"Well, I'm sure Hannah will be okay. After all, Poland is a long way away."

He watched as Annabelle froze.

"No, you do not understand. I have seen him here, in this village. His name is Jakub Baros, and he was Hannah's first boyfriend. Then Geoff came and took her from him. Jakub was very angry."

Perhaps the bloke David mentioned wasn't asking for me?

Ant patted Annabelle on the shoulder as if he were soothing a pet dog.

"Listen, I'll get Lyn to have a word with Hannah to keep an eye out and let us know if she sees anyone suspicious. It'll be fine, I'm sure."

Annabelle stiffened. Her face froze.

"Please, no. Do not tell Hannah he might be here. She will be very frightened. Jakub threatened Geoff when Hannah left Poland."

Before Ant could answer, his mobile rang.

"Ant, it's me. I'll have to put our meal tonight back by a couple of hours. Got to sort out my warring parents again. Meet you in the Wherry Arms just before nine instead of seven, okay?"

8

TRUE FRIENDS

"Where does everyone come from?" asked Ant as he fought his way through to a reserved table at the back of the snug.

Looking over his shoulder, he realised he'd been inadvertently talking to an elderly woman he didn't know who smiled sympathetically. Taking his seat, Ant didn't have long to wait before Sarah, one of the casual staff brought in on busy nights, approached.

"You've only just made it. The kitchen closes in ten minutes. Do you know what you want?"

Keen not to miss dinner, he looked at the specials board on the far wall and chose a main course for both himself and Lyn.

Hope she likes toad-in-the-hole.

A few minutes passed as Ant surveyed the organised chaos with staff and customers charging across the entrance to the tiny snug, most gawping at him as they passed.

Now I know what a goldfish feels like.

"Good heavens, here at last."

Ant's mood lifted as Lyn breezed into the small space,

followed by a barman carrying a pint of Fen Bodger pale ale and a white wine lemonade spritzer.

"I thought we'd be posh tonight," said Ant as Lyn settled herself into an old wooden chair opposite her friend. Sarah said they were closing the kitchen, so I ordered for you."

He waited for Lyn's inevitable response. It wasn't long coming.

"Remember last time you used your initiative to order me food? Well, if it's tripe and pickled onion again, it's going back this time—understand?"

Ant's eyes lit up.

"Aha, you underestimate me. I have a surprise."

I can see she doesn't believe me.

At that second, Sarah arrived with two steaming dishes in hand. Placing the meals on the table, she then stood back to admire the chef's work.

This isn't going well.

"Ant, since when has toad-in-the-hole and a white wine with lemonade been posh?"

He watched in silence as she eyed her plate with disdain. Ant lifted his pint and offered a toast.

"To fine food and good company."

Ant hated it when Lyn gave him a look she might offer to a six-year-old having had "a little accident."

At least I try.

Toast completed, the pair tucked into two overcooked meals. Ant made a point of commenting how good the food was. It was as if the more he said it, the more he believed his own assessment. He had the feeling the same couldn't be said for Lyn.

"Did you sort your parents out?" asked Ant, keen to move the subject away from stodgy Yorkshire pudding and sausages, which defied all but the most substantial of molars.

He allowed her the time to reply since he could see Lyn was having difficulty chewing her food sufficiently before it could be safely swallowed.

"Put it this way," said Lyn, picking a piece of gristle from her teeth. "If they were two of my young pupils, I'd sit them in a room until they saw sense."

Ant offered his sympathy. Lyn batted it away.

"They'll never change. I swear when the Grim Reaper comes, they'll accuse him of favouritism in choosing one to go before the other."

Lyn sighed before resuming battle with her meal.

Ant contented himself by emptying the last of his pint and attracting the barman's attention for a refill.

"Anyway, from the sublime to the ridiculous. Tell me about the meeting with your detective friend."

Ant playfully shook his head to acknowledge the absurdity of Lyn's comment while taking a first gulp from his new pint, then held the glass up to the light so he could admire the liquid gold.

"I refuse to ruin my pale ale by thinking of Plod in those terms," replied Ant in a lofty tone before laughing at his own pomposity.

"One thing is obvious though. He sees no connection between Geoff's body disappearing from the morgue and his cause of death. As for getting us pulled over on Sunday, nope, I don't believe it. He's either a good actor, or stupid. And I know which of the two I'll settle for."

Ant was aware of Lyn's studied look as he took another gulp of his pale ale.

"The thing is, Ant, do *you* see any connection?"

He placed his glass back onto the table with the reverence of an antiquarian mounting a precious artefact ready for close inspection.

"Let's put it this way, someone didn't want Geoff Singleton's body interfered with, which begs two questions: who and why?"

The reappearance of Sarah interrupted his flow.

"I've kept two slices of lemon cheesecake back for you, if you're in the mood?"

Ant smiled. Lyn licked her lips.

"Does that come with ice cream?" asked Ant.

"Frothy cream from a can for me," said Lyn.

Sarah touched the side of her nose.

"I'll see what I can do."

Sarah disappeared as quickly as she'd appeared, leaving the two friends to resume their analysis.

"As I see it, Lyn, there are three possible suspects: Hannah herself, though she'd have to have been a magnificent actor to carry it off, but not impossible. Then there's dear Rufus."

He could see Lyn was desperate to jump in.

"Well, you told me he knocked around with some dodgy characters. Perhaps the deal with Geoff went pear shaped, and Rufus wanted his money back—or worse?"

Ant rubbed his chin between two fingers.

"You're correct. Rufus is as mad as a box of frogs when the mood takes him. But kidnapping a body? I guess we won't know for sure until or unless he contacts Hannah demanding money for its safe return. But you know—"

"Hang on. That's two who might be in the frame. You said three?"

Ant smiled.

"Did I? Oh, yes, I did, didn't I? Well, there's Jakub Baros."

Lyn sat back in her chair and stared at her fellow sleuth.

"Who?" she said as if Ant had simply made the name up.

"Jakub Baros, Hannah's first love. Apparently, he's the jealous sort. What's more, he's been seen in the village."

Ant stemmed a flood of questions from Lyn by recounting his chance encounter with Annabelle.

"Did she describe what he looked like?"

Ant thought for a moment as he mentally ran through their conversation.

"A bit scruffy, and a scar."

Lyn banged her glass onto the table with such force that it gave Ant a start.

"I saw him yesterday, or rather, he almost knocked me over. And if he drives a four by four, we can put him at the boathouse on Saturday morning," replied Lyn as she told Ant about the damage to Irene Chapman's car.

Good eye for detail.

"You're learning, Lyn. Fabulous. All I can say is that Hannah's lucky to have a friend like Annabelle to watch her back."

Their eyes locked.

"You know what?" said Sarah, as she returned with the sweet. "The way you two look at each other, well, people might think you're an old married couple still mad about one other."

Ant frowned as he broke eye contact to engage Sarah.

"Married? That's for crazy people."

Ant turned back to Lyn and noted her gentle smile fading as she played with her glass, eyes now firmly fixed on the turning object.

9

BURNT OUT

"So there you are, Anthony. I was just talking to this young detective about the war. His father was at Monte Casino as part of the Italian campaign like me. Small world, isn't it?"

Ant couldn't disguise his surprise at finding Detective Inspector Riley in the library of Stanton Hall, let alone hear him being described as "young."

He greeted the smiling policeman politely enough. After all, that's how he had been brought up, but he felt uneasy as he tried to make sense of what the policeman was doing talking to his father.

"I mentioned to the Earl of Stanton that my dad went all the way through without so much as a scratch. Isn't that amazing?"

Ant gave a faint smile and nodded as he turned to a side table and poured a cup of coffee.

No visible scars, anyway.

"Well," said the earl, "I'll leave you two gentlemen to get on with things. I'm sure the detective has had quite enough of the ramblings of an old soldier."

Riley managed an embarrassed smile.

"Goodbye, Detective Inspector Riley, and thank you for the wonderful work your colleagues and you do in keeping us all safe."

You might well blush.

Ant escorted his father into the terrace conservatory and made sure he was safely seated before rejoining his visitor in the library.

"He's a remarkable man. Mine's the same. They don't make them like that anymore, do they?"

Ant nodded.

Maybe there's more to Riley than I give him credit for.

"His generation are certainly tough cookies, Inspector. Not surprising given the experiences they all went through."

Ant offered Riley a top-up of his coffee.

"They're all the same. War doesn't distinguish between high and low born, does it, Lord Stanton?"

Ant paused as he replenished Riley's drink, unsure if the detective had reverted to type, but gave Riley the benefit of doubt.

"As you say, Detective Inspector, war doesn't give a damn who it hurts."

The room fell into silence.

Riley glanced around his elaborate surroundings, seeming to linger on the more ornate features of a pair of bookcase cabinets.

Ant watched and waited.

Wait for it. One rule for the rich, another for the workers.

He was pleasantly surprised when the expected sarcasm didn't materialise.

"We traced the car that stopped you on Sunday."

"Really?" replied Ant, caught out that the detective had bothered to follow the matter up. "And the owner?"

"It was stolen, I'm afraid, so no trace there. We found it burnt out on an abandoned World War II airfield between Norwich and Cambridge."

Ant took a few seconds to digest the information and formulate where to go next. Taking Riley's empty china cup and saucer from his outstretched hand, he returned the delicate object to a veneered mahogany side table.

"Dare I ask about fingerprints?"

"As I said, the car was burnt to a crisp. We think a couple of local scallywags found it, took it for a spin before dumping and setting light to it."

"Then how did you come to find it?"

Riley smiled, which was not something Ant had seen him do often.

"A coincidence, and good police work. Over recent months, we've had reports of kids using laser pens to distract pilots. We asked the aviation authority to let us know about any incidents they receive from aircrew. We got one such report earlier this week. We followed it up, and hey, presto..."

It wasn't often Ant felt compelled to congratulate the detective. He felt the need to do so now.

"What can I say? But why are you going to so much trouble if it was just kids who torched the car?"

Ant's question was framed to drag as much information from Riley as possible.

"Well, as you mentioned to me the other day, whoever stopped you knew quite a bit about your background."

"Are you any nearer to finding out who he was?" replied Ant, eager for any clue the detective might unwittingly provide.

Riley took a step back, turned, and began to make his way to the door.

"We're working on that. I should also just mention that I expect you to contact me immediately should you hear anything about the whereabouts of Geoffrey Singleton's body. Do we understand each other?"

Just can't help himself.

"ANTHONY, Lyn is on the telephone. Don't keep the girl waiting."

The Earl of Stanton's voice carried down the long gallery of Stanton Hall without Ant's father having to raise his voice.

"Got it, Dad," replied Ant as he lifted the receiver.

"Ant, I've just taken a call from Hannah. She sounds terrified."

"What's wrong?"

"She says she's seen Jakub Baros peering into her front window. I've sent Tina round to keep her company. Shall I ring the police?"

Ant knew he had to act quickly.

"Where's Annabelle?"

"Hannah garbled something about her having to fly back to Poland to arrange finance for some building conversion project."

"Okay," replied Ant. "That makes sense. Annabelle told me she wanted to buy the old Methodist hall. I guess that's what she's on about. Don't ring the police. I'll shoot over straight away."

ANT ARRIVED to find Tina fussing over Hannah, trying to get

the woman to drink tea. The traumatised woman sat in a far corner of the large room shaking like a leaf as she stared through a picture window onto the front garden.

"What's been going on?"

Tina shrugged her shoulders.

"Lyn asked me to come over, and this is what I found. I've had a quick look around outside, but I can't see anyone."

Ant noticed a short length of old wood about two inches square resting on the arm of a chair.

"Just as well you didn't find him, Hannah." Ant smiled as he pointed to the timber.

His effort to lift her mood failed. There was no reaction.

"Look at me," said Ant quietly as he knelt down beside Hannah. His persistence paid off. Eventually, she made eye contact.

"Good." His calm, gentle voice began to tease Hannah from her stupor.

"Tell me about this Jakub chap. It's safe, don't worry. We won't leave you alone."

Ant watched Hannah tense at the mention of her old flame's name.

"I promise you; I won't let anything happen to you. Annabelle told me the pair of you were fond of each other when you were younger. Yes?"

He could tell that being taken back in time had a curiously cathartic effect on Hannah. For a few seconds, her facial features relaxed. The moment soon passed.

"Yes, you are correct. He was my first serious boyfriend. We lived in a small village, and he was very handsome."

Ant smiled, urging Hannah to continue.

"But as we got older, he started to get into trouble. Small things at first then more serious. He met some bad people.

And if he thought I had looked at another boy, he got very angry. One time he hit..."

Hannah's voice tailed off, and tears began to flow.

It's okay to remember. Let it out.

"And Geoff?" Ant worked hard to help Hannah maintain eye contact.

That's it, Hannah. Come on, smile. It's okay to remember the good times with those we grieve for.

"He came to the village one day. I was down at the harbour, and he had come to look at a boat. He bumped into me. I think he did it on purpose." Hannah broke into a broad smile. "And that was it. We were inseparable. But Jakub..."

Her voice began to tremble as she spoke his name.

Ant knew he'd pushed things as far as he could.

"Listen," said Ant, getting to his feet, "why don't I have a look around while you get a few things together. I've spoken to Lyn. She thinks it might be a good idea for you to spend a couple of days at her place. It's right in the centre of the village with plenty of people around. It beats being stuck here in the middle of nowhere, don't you think?"

Ant observed a small nod. That was enough to confirm arrangements.

10

COLD COMFORT

Ant's quad bike roared to life as he pressed the engine start button and twisted the throttle. In seconds, the machine had crossed Stanton Hall's shingle courtyard and raced into the open countryside.

As he took in the view of the family's land, he remembered a time when he'd found it difficult coming to terms with the privileges he enjoyed. This was balanced by the memory of his parents' decision not to send him to preparatory school but to the local primary.

I hated being the odd one out.

Ribbed mercilessly by most of the other kids, he knew his parents had been right to ensure he experienced the real world. Some of those children now worked for the estate just as their parents had. Others left the village and went on to professional careers. His best friend, Lyn Blackthorn, was a case in point. She'd left to get away from her warring parents, worked hard for her degree, and returned to the village as a head teacher.

He, too, had felt the need to escape after the death of his older brother and the responsibilities that would eventually fall to him. As he pondered the future of the business, the finances of which didn't make for restful sleep, he watched two figures scurrying about on the roof of one of the estate's Victorian follies.

He was too far away to make out who they were. However, given the remote location, he knew they had to be locals.

Well, I'll be damned. They're stripping the lead.

In his youth he'd have jumped into the fray. Now he took a more measured approach. If military conflict had taught him anything, it was that rushing into a situation without weighing up the options usually ended badly.

Not exactly an armed threat, but here we go.

Ant cut the engine and allowed the quad bike to coast the final hundred yards down a gentle slope to the edge of a clearing from where he could keep his unwanted visitors under observation.

Two teenagers skipped across the steep pitch of the obelisk like a pair of mountain gazelles. Even though they were damaging a building of historical value, he couldn't help but admire their athleticism.

About fifteen I'd say.

Dismounting the bike, Ant crept up on their blind side until he stood at the foot of the flint-faced construction. As he heard one of them sliding down to the eaves in preparation to jump, Ant stepped back so he could confront the intruder.

"Good morning, young man. Can I help you with that? It must be heavy?"

The sound of Ant's authoritative voice caused the youth to shout in terror for his mum. Both youth and lead dropped from the eaves onto a lush carpet of long meadow grass.

Ant turned his gaze from the dishevelled youth rubbing

the hand his loot had fallen onto, to his accomplice, who was peering over the roof's edge to investigate the kerfuffle.

"Nice to meet you too, young lady. Do come and join us. Would you like a hand?"

Ant offered the girl an outstretched hand to ease her descent. Dismissing his offer, she leaped clear and landed next to her partner in crime.

"I hesitate to ask the obvious, but what exactly are you doing?"

The would-be thieves glanced at each other, then the lead, and finally at Ant.

Your faces really are a picture.

"Fair enough. I suppose that was a stupid question."

The youths scrunched their faces as if competing in a gurning competition.

"What's he on about?" muttered the boy.

"He's mad. Who is he, anyway?" replied the girl without bothering to look at the adult towering over them.

Top marks for bravado.

He remembered being their age. One which excluded adults from having anything of interest to say and whose only function was to shout and make teenagers' lives a misery.

"An apt enquiry, young lady. I'm the man whose family owns the ground you're sitting on. Oh, and the lead you kindly thought to relieve us of."

The youths turned to look at the alloy resting forlornly in the long grass, then at Ant.

"If you own this lot, you're not going to miss a bit of lead, are you?" The girl nodded in an act of solidarity with her more forward accomplice.

"True, but that isn't the point—"

"It's okay for you. You're rich, right? We've got nothing.

No money or any chance of a job. There isn't anything for us around here. My dad says the rich get richer, and the poor stay poor."

Well, that told me.

He observed the pair for a few seconds, their eyes locked on his. Neither had used bad language, given him backchat, or tried to run for it. Instead, they were standing, or rather sitting, their ground.

"Well, what *do* you want to do with your lives?"

His question met with two sets of shrugging shoulders and four eyes inspecting their respective owner's scuffed trainers.

"Nothing. You'll drop us in it with the police. They'll take us to court, and the judge will let us off and tell us not to do it again. It's always the same."

Ant's irritation surfaced.

"Is that so, young man? Then get off your backsides and do something about it. Or are you both more comfortable playing the victim, always choosing to blame others, and thinking of a dozen reasons why you can't do something to help yourselves?"

He waited and watched as the teenagers looked at their mobiles, deciding if they should bother to respond.

"Listen. I'm not interested in the police. I had my own issues with them when I was younger, so I'm hardly going to set them on you."

The teenagers looked up from their screens and frowned. Adult interest was not something they were used to.

"Let's try this again. What do you want to do with your lives?"

The girl answered first, albeit hesitantly.

"A mechanic."

I think you've just blown your mate away.

Emboldened, the boy joined in.

"Working with animals."

Now it was her turn to look surprised.

Ant smiled, careful not to appear patronising.

"Something tells me that's the first time either of you have talked to anyone about your ambitions."

Neither responded.

"Okay, give me your mobile numbers, help me put the lead back on the roof, and we'll say no more about it. I promise you; I'll have a word with one or two people to see if there's anyone that might have an opening. Do we have a deal?"

Your smile tells me we do.

FOR GOODNESS' sake Fitch, go on.

Ant stood back amused as his friend stared nervously at the half-open doors to the painted steel shipping container.

"I've been in once, remember. That was enough." Fitch began to shuffle backwards until he bumped into Ant and let out a shriek in terror.

Ant gently pushed his friend forward and shook his head.

"Don't be daft. He's dead. What do you think he's going to do? Sit up and ask you how much you charge for a full service? Anyway, since you dragged me away from watching the football, tell me again just how you ended up in the middle of nowhere with a dead bloke?"

Fitch turned his back on the container, after having one last peek at the lumpy, white shroud at the far end of the dark space.

"Well, I got a call to fix a diesel generator."

"From a bloke you'd never heard of, saying he'd pay a hundred and fifty pounds cash, which you'd find under an oil drum inside the generator room, right?"

You might well blush.

"I know it sounds daft, but I thought it was easy money for an hour's work."

Ant listened in disbelief as Fitch retold the events that had brought him to the back end of Brinton Fen on a sticky Thursday afternoon.

"Daft? That's putting it mildly. Anyway, how did you come to poke your nose in the container?"

Fitch turned and pointed to a shabby brick building twenty yards to their left.

"I turned up and followed the bloke's instructions. Sure enough, I found the generator—and my money. I got stuck in and soon found a couple of loose connections. That's all there was to it. I cleaned up the leads, tightened them, and switched her on."

Ant waited for more.

"And then what?"

"What do you mean? It started, of course. What did you expect?"

Ant pointed towards the container.

"And the corpse?"

He noticed Fitch shudder at the mention of the body.

"A bit of bad luck, really."

You're telling me.

"Bad luck? At least you're still breathing, unlike your friend covered in a white sheet, surrounded by two-dozen boxes of frozen peas in a big tin box with wonky wiring."

From Fitch's reaction, Ant guessed his friend was trying to think of anything but dead people.

"Assuming the job was done, I started to make my way back to the van when I saw a red light flashing on the side of the container and heard an alarm sounding."

Ant gestured towards the container.

"And curiosity got the better of you?"

Oops, touched his sensibilities there.

"It's not a case of curiosity. I'm a professional, I am. There was no alarm before I fixed the generator. There was one after I switched it on. I figured the freezer temperature monitor needed resetting, and I was right."

Ant scanned the side of the container for the control panel. Unable to see it, he turned to Fitch, who was wearing a wry smile.

"No, it's inside, which is how I came to find—"

"Simon the stiff."

Fitch frowned.

"If you say so."

Ant grinned, pleased at his own joke.

"Talking of whom, Fitch, we'd better have a look at the frozen one, then get the hell out of here. I wager the man who hired you won't be too pleased if he finds out we know what's in here."

Fitch once more began to step away from the corrugated steel doors.

"I've told you. I'm not going in there again. Seeing the anaemic soles of that bloke's feet last time was enough for me."

Gesturing for his friend to stand aside, Ant stepped into the container and gently pulled back a sheet covering the body.

"Good Lord. It's Geoff Singleton."

11
PARALLEL UNIVERSE

"Are you sure this is a good idea?"

Ant looked over his shoulder at Lyn as he rinsed his empty coffee cup under the hot tap.

"Listen, Fitch was the one that started this caper. If he hadn't been so keen to earn a bit of cash in hand, we wouldn't need to explain anything to 'Inspector Clouseau of Witless Yard.'"

Ant's parody of Riley speaking in a fake French accent was enough to make Lyn choke on her drink.

"Not bad for you, Anthony Stanton. Not bad at all," she said, wiping a dribble of coffee from her chin.

"And what has the corpse-finder general had to say on the matter?"

Ant could see Fitch still looked unsettled from his afternoon's work.

"Not funny, Ant."

Lyn sympathised by putting an arm around her friend.

"Never you mind the nasty aristocrat. I'm on your side. It must have been a nasty shock. But can I just ask if you managed to bring any of those peas back, only I'm a bit short."

Get in there, girl.

Having lulled Fitch into a false sense of security, Lyn's apparent afterthought did the trick. All three broke into a chorus of laughter, compounded by Ant spending the following few minutes prancing around Lyn's farmhouse kitchen doing a terrible impersonation of Peter Sellers as the famous French detective, while Lyn took on the mantle of Kato Fong, his faithful retainer, by leaping from various hiding places to demonstrate his martial arts skills on his employer.

"Where did you to learn that?" said Ant as he nursed a sore wrist from Lyn having twisted it during one of her more successful attacks.

Lyn smiled enigmatically.

"A girl can't be too careful these days, so I've been attending Cybil Dawson's self-defence classes for women. Two pounds seventy-five a session including ginger-nut biscuits and orange squash."

Ant huffed.

"Cybil Dawson? She's seventy-five if she's a day, and limps around the village leaning on a barley-twist walking stick,"

I knew it; Lyn has gone mad.

Lyn stepped slowly forward and smiled as she took hold of Ant's left hand. Confused, he smiled back, before wincing in pain as she applied one of Cybil's special restraint techniques for repelling unwanted advances.

The more Ant cried out, the more pressure Lyn applied, until he dropped to his knees and pleaded for mercy.

"Nothing to do with age or strength come to that," said Lyn as she towered above her adversary. "As a matter of fact,

Cybil took down a pickpocket in London last summer. He made the mistake of confusing infirmity with vulnerability."

"And..." said Fitch, who had been consoling himself scoffing a piece of Lyn's renowned lemon cheesecake.

"Three days in hospital with a broken arm and three months in prison for aggravated assault," replied Lyn without taking a breath.

"Who, the pickpocket, or Cybil?" replied Ant, confused and still smarting from a painful wrist.

"Funny," replied Lyn while giving Ant a sideways glance.

"I'm being seri—"

His protest was cut short by the sound of the doorbell.

"He's here," said Fitch.

Lyn broke off the conversation and headed for the front door.

"And don't say anything you know I will have a go at you later for." Ant watched Fitch frown, his confusion obvious. "Oh, don't look so daft. Just don't tell Riley anything he doesn't need to know, yes?"

Saints preserve us all.

The pair listened intently as Lyn went through the pleasantries of welcoming Riley and bidding him to follow her into the kitchen.

"Finding the same body twice. That's a record, even for you."

Ant's natural instinct was to challenge Riley's sarcastic comment, except he'd promised Lyn to be on his best behaviour.

The unlikely foursome sat around Lyn's rectangular dining table in a seating configuration that made it plain it was three against one.

"As I said, Detective Inspector, strictly speaking, it wasn't me who found Geoff Singleton's body, it was my friend here."

Riley's eyes turned toward Fitch, who wriggled on the hard seat as if he had ants in his pants.

"I don't know what else I can tell you?" said Fitch. "I went to fix a generator, saw a red light flashing and opened the container doors, and there it... I mean he, was."

Fitch shrugged his shoulders and looked anywhere except at the detective.

Riley scrutinised each of the friends in turn, lingering longest on Ant. After what seemed an age, the detective sat back in his chair.

"The police service thanks you for bringing this matter to its attention. I think that will be all for now."

Riley got to his feet.

Something not right here. What's he up to?

Ant attempted to draw Riley out.

"So what's next, Detective Inspector?"

Riley looked down at Ant.

"Next?"

You know what I mean, fool.

"It means we get the post-mortem done before some light-fingered villain nicks the body again. You don't get any prizes for finding him a third time. Unless, of course you'd like some jail time?"

Ant sensed an opportunity to wind his foe up.

"What, you mean like that bloke who Cybil Dawson took down with her barley-twist walking stick in London?"

Ant adopted a look of faux horror.

"London? Walking Stick? And who on earth is Cybil Dawson?" replied Riley in a tone tinged with exasperation.

"Don't mind my friend," said Lyn. "He's been on the

chocolate, which makes him stupid until the e-numbers wear off."

Ant noted Lyn's indifference as he attempted to stare the detective out, who, to his disappointment, soon tired of Ant's provocation.

"As a matter of fact, it's happening right now, and I'm confident it will prove Mr Singleton died from natural causes. I'm sure you are aware he had a serious health condition?"

Lyn opened her mouth as if to speak. Ant anticipated what was coming next and tapped her shin under the table.

Lyn jumped in surprise, drawing a bemused look from Riley.

"Were you about to say something, or is it your habit to make random sounds for no apparent reason?"

Lyn bit her lip to take her mind off the pain.

I'll pay for that.

"Good riddance to him, I say," said Fitch as Lyn closed the front door and made her way back into the kitchen.

"You two are nuts; you know that, don't you? One of these days Riley's going to get you."

Ant laughed.

"He's too stupid."

Lyn tossed an apple at Ant from a bowl of fruit on the worktop.

"Not so stupid that you were worried over what I was about to say to him."

Ant executed a nifty sidestep to his left allowing the Norfolk Royal to whizz past his shoulder and bounce off the bread bin onto the floor.

"If you mean hand him information on a plate, you're correct."

Lyn huffed.

"Anyway, who's for another coffee?"

"Good move, Ant," said Fitch as he handed over his empty mug.

Lyn giggled as she watched Ant trying to work out how the percolator worked. Round one went to the machine, causing Ant to leave the room in a huff on the pretext of retrieving something from his car.

Fitch took the opportunity to quiz Lyn.

"How are things between you two? I'm guessing all this shin kicking and apple throwing is displacement activity for, you know, getting it together?"

Fitch's perceptive comments took Lyn by surprise.

"What on earth do you mean?"

Fitch walked over to the percolator and prepared it for a fresh brew before switching the machine on.

"Come off it. I know I'm a bloke, but even I can see what's going on... or rather, what's *not* going on."

"Who's not doing what?" said Ant as he re-entered the room holding a small screwdriver.

Fitch brushed Ant's enquiry aside, advising his friend he had no need of the screwdriver.

"How did you do that?" asked Ant as he glimpsed the red "on" light of the percolator, forgetting about his earlier question.

"I pressed the button marked 'on.' It's not complicated, you know."

Ant peered at the machine as if it had conspired with the others to make him look stupid.

"Come and sit down," said Lyn, holding out her hand.

Ant surprised himself by gently taking Lyn's fingers while lowering himself onto a chair next to her.

"Here's what I think about the body snatcher. It seems to

me that there are only two possibilities, assuming we dismiss the notion Geoff died of natural causes."

"Go on," said Ant, keen to see if her assessment matched his own.

"Well, either Hannah arranged it to stop his corpse being cut up—"

"Or?" interrupted Ant.

"Or whoever murdered him stole the body to stop the post-mortem unearthing how they killed him."

"Exactly," added Lyn, her face beaming as she realised they agreed for once.

"And that person looks to be Jakub Baros, Lyn, yes?"

Fitch reached for the percolator and poured three coffees.

"Of course, the two could be linked," said Fitch.

Ant gestured for another sugar to be dropped into his coffee.

"That's what I've just said."

Ant wiped coffee splashes from his wrist as the sugar cube Fitch had released landed with a plop.

"No, you mentioned two people with different motives, Ant. How about if Hannah's apparent terror of her old flame is an act, and they're actually in it together?"

Ant smiled.

"Interesting. In that case it's worth me doing some digging around this Jakub fellow."

"And I'll have a chat with Hannah after school tomorrow to see if she gives anything away."

12

OLD MACDONALD

"Thank goodness that's it for another week. This term always feels the longest," said Lyn as she followed Hannah into her large rear garden. "You're nice and secluded here, that's for sure. Good to hide away from the world sometimes, isn't it?"

Lyn's line of conversation wasn't meant to offer any deep insight into the merits of privacy. Her intention was to get her to talk.

Wish I could read your thoughts.

Hannah looked pensive as they settled into a pair of matching faux bamboo chairs protected from the strong sunlight by a huge parasol.

"It's good of you to spend so much of your time with me." She spoke in a quiet voice, without making eye contact with Lyn, who rested a reassuring hand on Hannah's arm.

"Not at all. I can't begin to understand what you're going through, so I won't use the silly words most people splutter because they don't know what to say."

Hannah smiled and stole a look at Lyn from beneath her auburn fringe.

"You have a very important job, I think. Many responsibilities for all those little children."

Lyn returned the smile, pleased that Hannah was beginning to open up.

"Oh, I don't know. I have a good team of teachers and support staff. The place runs itself really. As for the children, well, they're fine. Unfortunately, I can't say the same for some of the parents."

Hannah wagged a playful finger.

"I think you are too modest."

Lyn tried not to blush.

"I'm not sure some of the parents share that view, but we all rub along together somehow."

Hannah began to frown then relaxed as she processed Lyn's line of self-deprecation.

"Ah, one of your strange English sayings, 'rub along.' Yes, I understand."

Lyn's approach was starting to pay dividends. Hannah's body language was more open now. Instinctively, Lyn mirrored it.

Time to push, I think.

"Has the detective been in touch recently?"

Hannah's smile slipped as the outside world started to once more intrude.

"No, but the, how you say, liaison officer, has. She has told me about Geoff. It is horrible, but I understand they have to find out how he died."

Lyn decided not to ask if Hannah knew the exact details of where her husband's body was found. She saw no need to add to her misery.

"You're right. Knowing what actually happened will help you eventually. We can deal with things we know about. It's uncertainty that is the hardest thing to bear, isn't it?"

Hannah nodded then stood up and headed for the kitchen door.

"I have some wonderful fruit cordial. A recipe my mother taught me back in Poland. I will fetch some."

Keep yourself busy, that's the ticket.

She returned a few minutes later with two glass tumblers filled to the brim with a colourful liquid.

"Hmm, that's superb, Hannah." Lyn licked her lips as she sampled the iced drink.

"We always made it on hot days. It was one of Geoff's favourites."

Lyn remained silent, instead, allowing the stillness of the afternoon to do its work.

"You think something bad happened to my husband, don't you?"

Better get this reply right.

"The truth is, Hannah, no one knows. But yes, it's a possibility, no matter what the police say."

Hannah nodded as she lowered her head into her hands.

Go on, give yourself permission to think the unthinkable.

"So it's important we go on until we get to the truth, no matter where it takes us. That way we're doing it for Geoff. Isn't that right, Hannah?"

A few seconds of inactivity was broken by a nod of the head. It was enough for Lyn to know Hannah understood.

"Have you heard anything from Jakub?"

Lyn waited for Hannah to react. It wasn't long coming. As she raised her head, she stiffened and stared into the middle distance.

"Do you think he did this terrible thing? He shouted at Geoff very much when we came away."

Lyn searched for the right words to move the conversation forward, trying to sound positive.

"Ant is looking for him right now, but if you can be brave enough to tell me a bit more about the man, it might just make the difference when Ant, or the police, catch up with him."

Hannah remained silent. Lyn tried a different tack.

"Tell me about when you were both young. When you first met. He was your first real boyfriend, wasn't he?"

Hannah eventually warmed to Lyn's enquiry. Her words stirred long-lost memories of happier times.

"Annabelle told you, didn't she?" said Hannah. "It's okay, yes, they were good times. It was so exciting. You know, the first time a boy kisses you."

Lyn smiled; she had her own memories.

I should remind Ant of stolen kisses on his father's wherry.

"He was very handsome and funny. He brought me flowers from the meadow each Sunday during the summer. I think many of the girls in the village were jealous, but I didn't care. I was in love. But now…"

Lyn moved quickly to stop Hannah retreating back into herself.

"Just remember you are safe, and Ant will find Jakub. He won't get anywhere near you, I promise."

Hannah offered an unconvincing smile.

Think I've pushed hard enough for today.

Lyn allowed the silence to continue for a few seconds before getting up from her chair and offering Hannah a comforting touch.

"Well, looks to me like it's time to leave you in peace to enjoy the last of the sun with your wonderful cordial. Don't forget, Hannah, if you need anything, anything at all, or something happens that you don't like the look of, call me. I can be around in five minutes. Okay?"

Hannah nodded without making eye contact as Lyn walked towards the garden gate and out into the driveway.

"How are you doing, Lil? Can I have one of your lovely quarter pounders please with all the trimmings?"

Lil greeted Ant like the old friend he was.

"A good job I don't rely on you for my profits. Haven't seen you in ages. Where have you been hiding?"

Ant smiled and deflected the question as he stood at the village institution that was Lil's greasy spoon mobile chuck wagon. The battered old van had stood in its lay-by location for more years than he could remember. Nevertheless, she still served the best roadside food for miles around.

"Beautiful day," said Ant as he sniffed the delicious aroma of beef being fried on a small hotplate and looked out across a lush landscape towards the North Sea.

"I bet the wind gets at you during the winter?" said Ant as he continued to evade talking about himself.

Lil laughed.

"Don't remind me. My bones are getting too old for those easterlies. Go right through you, don't they?"

Lil passed Ant his steaming snack, piled high with cheese and fried onions.

"I know what you mean." Ant bit into the burger so enthusiastically that clear juices began to run down the sides of his mouth.

"Good?"

"Never better." Ant grinned as he took another great bite from his brunch.

If there was one thing that stopped Ant talking, it was good food. In the case of Lil's cuisine, it meant he failed to utter a word for the five minutes it took him to polish the burger off. In that time, he'd watched Lil scraping the hotplate clean with a stainless-steel spatula, and butter two-dozen buns in preparation for the lunchtime rush.

Wiping his face with a paper towel and brushing a patchwork of breadcrumbs from the front of his jacket, his attention turned to the subject of Jakub Baros.

"I don't suppose you've come across any strangers around the place over the last week or so?"

Lil gave a broad smile.

"What, you mean more so than my regulars?"

Ant nodded and returned her grin.

"I get your point. I just—"

"Although," Lil interrupted, "there was that chap who could have done with a good wash."

I wonder.

"I don't suppose he had a scar on one cheek, did he?"

Lil's face lit up.

"How did you know that? As a matter of fact, he did. When he ordered... well, I say ordered, he just pointed at the menu and shoved a twenty-pound note at me. Never seen anyone eat a double beef burger with bacon so fast in all my life. The man disappeared before I could give him his change." Lil pointed to a shelf behind her. "It's still waiting for him."

The two old friends shared a joke about the eating habits of men, before Ant pressed Lil for more detail.

"Did you notice a car or where he seemed to head for?"

Ant's question was asked more in hope than expectation.

Lil smiled again.

"As a matter of fact, I did. It was a clapped-out Skoda campervan with foreign number plates. You should have seen the muck its exhaust chucked out, something awful it was."

"You're sure it was a Skoda and not a Range Rover?"

Lil frowned.

"I think I know the difference between the two, young Mr Anthony. Anyway, he's parked up at the old piggery on Lane End Farm. It's been abandoned for years, so I suppose the lad will get a bit of quiet. I only know because I happened to follow it for a bit on my way home yesterday."

Ant leant over the high counter of the chuck wagon and placed a kiss on Lil's cheek.

"You're a corker, Lil. I need to speak to that lad, so I'll be saying cheerio and strike while the iron's hot."

"In that case you won't mind giving him his change for me, will you?" replied Lil, reaching over to the shelf to retrieve the cash.

With that he was gone, with Lil's voice telling him "not to leave it so long next time" still ringing in his ears. Loose shingle spat from the wheels of Ant's car as he left the lay-by for the main road and took a sharp right onto a narrow farm trackway. Although plain to see the track wasn't used often, he noticed newly fallen twigs and leaves scattered on the surface of the roadway.

Something big has been down here recently to cause this damage.

A few minutes later, the overgrown vegetation gave way to a scene of dereliction. As he brought the Morgan to a halt and climbed out of the car, he realised Lil had been right to say the farm had been left unoccupied for years. As he scrambled over collapsed walls, piles of old timber, and rusted metal cladding, he scanned the area for signs of life.

Out of nowhere, a foreign-sounding voice carried across the scene of devastation.

"What you want?"
Seconds seeming like hours followed in silence.
Then the voice again. This time much, much closer.
"What you want in this place?"
Ant felt clammy breathing on the nape of his neck.

He was also aware of a sharp object resting menacingly between his shoulder blades.

13

NUMBERS

"I don't suppose your name is Jakub Baros, by any chance?"

Ant's calming tone had an immediate effect as he felt the pressure from the object pressing into his back ease off.

Turning to face the stranger, Ant knew he'd found his man.

"You police?"

Ant studied the gruff-looking man, aged around thirty, with a mop of black, curly hair and a scar on his cheek.

Lil was right about him needing a bath.

"Perhaps you would like to put your knife down, now?" Ant concentrated on looking and sounding relaxed. This was no time for sudden movements.

"How you know my name?" His eyes scanned the derelict farmyard nervously.

Rather than answer Jakub's question, Ant pointed to the old campervan, which was parked behind a half-demolished cowshed so that just the front of the rusting vehicle was visible.

"Do you have insurance for that?"

Convinced now that Ant was a policeman, Jakub dropped the knife.

"It is mine, yes. I have proof—papers. It is legal."

Ant stood aside as Jakub hurried towards the campervan and retrieved a black, imitation leather folder from the glove compartment.

"See. I have insurance." He held out a piece of paper, which Ant scrutinised closely.

A shame I can't read Polish.

"This seems to be in order." Ant's tone was polite, but officious as he returned the document to Jakub, who nervously slipped it back into the plastic folder.

He's shaking.

"You go now? I have many things to do."

Ant's body language and tone made it clear that it was he to decide when it was time to leave.

"Norfolk is a long way from, er, where did you say you came from?"

Jakub's eyes narrowed. He glanced at the knife lying amongst a pile of broken roof tiles and twisted metal. Ant followed the man's glance.

"I don't think we'll be needing this today, do you?" He bent down and retrieved the blade, admiring the quality of its manufacture.

Jakub didn't move.

"A small fishing village near Lublin."

Looks almost relieved I've taken control of the knife.

Ant suspected the man's temper had got him in trouble before. At least this time the temptation had been removed. He gestured for Jakub to follow him across the yard. As Jakub turned to see where he was pointing, Ant took the opportunity to throw the knife in the opposite direction.

"We know quite a lot about you. Do you know a woman called Hannah Singleton?"

Jakub bristled at the mention of her name.

Is he going to run for it or stay to find out what I really know?

"Do join me," Ant said, inviting Jakub to sit with him on a set of stone steps leading to the upper floor of what was once a sizeable grain store. His quiet voice did the trick.

Looks like he isn't going anywhere.

Jakub sat down, his body odour making Ant wonder if he been a little too accommodating in his offer.

"Tell me about Hannah. She was your girlfriend, yes?"

Jakub shrugged his shoulders.

"You know this already. Why do you ask?"

Ant pressed his point.

"Because, Jakub, her husband was murdered a few days ago. Then again you already know that, don't you?"

Jakub attempted to get up. Ant placed a firm hand on the man's arm to dissuade him.

"Hannah called me saying she was in trouble and for me to come. She needed my help. So I come." Jakub shrugged his shoulders again as he submitted to Ant's firm restraint. "And now, nothing. I call. She does not answer. I go to house. She is not there. What am I to do?"

What on earth is going on?

"You're telling me you came all the way from Poland because of a telephone call, and now the woman who rang you won't see or speak to you? Sorry, that doesn't make sense."

Ant felt Jakub tensing.

He's either going to hit me or make a run for it.

"I have told you; Hannah is in trouble. You say you know

everything about me. So you know how special that lady is to me, okay?"

One of them is a very good liar, but which one?

Jakub picked up a small shard of rusty metal and began twisting the material. Ant quickly understood what the man's actions might lead to.

Better keep him talking.

"Listen, I'm here to help you. We know you were jealous when Geoff took Hannah away. Who wouldn't be? Most men have had those feelings. But Geoffrey Singleton is dead, and you have suddenly appeared out of nowhere. I don't think you had anything to do with his murder, but you must help me. Do you understand?"

Oops, shouldn't have mentioned 'murder.'

Ant made no attempt to stop Jakub as the man sprang from the steps and put ten feet between them. He knew the next few seconds would end in one of three ways:

Jakub would launch an attack.

He would run for it.

He'd see sense and stay put.

That was a close-run thing, mused Ant as Jakub paused, turned to look at the campervan, then back at Ant and put his clenched fists in the pockets of his work-worn, black leather jacket.

"Hannah called me on Tuesday. She was crying. It was hard to understand her. She said they had been arguing for weeks and were breaking up, but then Geoff died." He allowed his shoulders to rest forward and stared at the debris beneath his feet.

Good man. Stay where you are.

"She said she was being blamed for his death, and the police were going to do something to his body, then take her away."

Ant remained seated. He spoke in a calm, measured tone.

"Didn't that seem strange to you?"

Jakub frowned.

"But it was Hannah. If she said something is so, then it is so."

Love is a terrible thing sometimes.

"She said I should hide his body until she could prove her innocence."

Ant got to his feet and closed the distance between them.

"You mean Hannah told you where his body was, how to get Geoff out of the mortuary, and where to hide him?"

Is she taking us for mugs?

"You said she called you? Then you will have her number saved on your mobile?"

Jakub rummaged through the pocket of his coat. From the time it took him to retrieve the phone, Ant assumed the lining had perished.

"It is always the same; she never answers," replied Jakub as he handed an ancient mobile over.

Ant looked at the call log. Baros seemed to be telling the truth. He also noted a long list of unanswered calls the other way.

He's certainly been persistent.

"And you still don't think it's a bit funny?" said Ant as he tried the number twice without success.

Jakub screwed up his face. Ant realised his error.

"Sorry, I didn't mean it like a joke. What I meant was it's a bit strange. Do you understand?"

Jakub's facial features relaxed.

"But I love her. What she asks for, I do."

Is love that blind, or is he having me over?

"She still loves me. I know this. She told me to be careful because the police were watching. You are here. She tells me the truth."

Time to check a few things out.

"You will stay here until I send for you Jakub. Do you understand?" Ant slipped Jakub's mobile into his pocket. He was relieved the stranger made no attempt to stop him.

"Understand?" repeated Ant.

Jakub nodded.

Right, let's get to the bottom of this.

14

NO HIDING PLACE

Saturday morning broke with a fine drizzle, which left the grasslands of Stanton Hall glistening against a shy sun peeping out from a huge bank of dark grey clouds.

"You're out and about early," said Ant as he watched Lyn cover the last few yards from the lawn in front of the Hall and across the gravel driveway to the double front doors.

She handed Ant a round tin as she scrubbed her wellington boots on the coconut doormat before stepping into the majestic hallway.

"Thought it would be good exercise since I sit at a desk for most of the week. And by the way, don't pinch any of that chocolate cake before your mum and dad have had some. Your butler told me what you did last week."

Ant adopted his best schoolboy "it wasn't me" look as he gently shook the tin to check how big the cake might be.

"To be fair, the cook thought the tin was empty and put it in the pantry."

Lyn seized her opportunity.

"Since when does a fully qualified cook store empty tins in the larder?"

Ant tried to rebuff Lyn's logic.

"I was hungry."

Lyn shook her head.

"What, to scoff enough Victoria sponge to start a cake stall?"

The banter continued as the two friends passed into the morning room of the Tudor building.

Time to change the subject, I think.

"Anyway, enough about cake, how did you get on with Hannah yesterday?"

Lyn took the bait as the pair settled themselves into a matching pair of Chippendale chairs.

"She told me all about this Jakub Baros chap. It seems he has a temper and mixed with some dodgy types when he was younger. Hannah said he'd been in trouble for violence, and she was frightened of him."

"Interesting," replied Ant as he rubbed his chin in the style of Sherlock Holmes.

Lyn's look of irritation told Ant he needed to expand.

"Well, Hannah may not be as innocent as she makes out. In fact, there's a good chance she's one of the best actors either of us has come across."

Lyn shook her head.

"If you're thinking she had anything to do with her husband's death, you're on the wrong track. I've spent a lot of time with her over the last few days, and I can tell you her grief is genuine."

Ant offered Lyn a mint from a small silver dish on the veneered mahogany coffee table, which separated their chairs.

"I accept her tears may be genuine. The question is, for whom is she weeping. Geoff or herself?"

Lyn took the mint and popped it into her already open mouth.

"You clearly know something I don't, so out with it, clever clogs."

Ant spent the next few minutes filling Lyn in about his run-in with Jakub the previous day.

"You see, either he's a fantastic actor, or she's been manipulating him. Believe me, two minutes in his company is enough to convince anyone he's not the sharpest chisel in the toolbox."

Lyn leant forward in her chair to pick up a second mint from the small silver dish.

"So we have a jealous ex-boyfriend, with known violent tendencies, showing up just when the body of his love's rival gets himself bumped off. Have I missed anything?"

Got it in one.

"Congratulations, Lyn. You've won our Sleuth of the Month competition, and first prize is as many mints as you can eat in five minutes."

"The only problem is," said Lyn, ignoring his attempt at humour and beginning to suck on the sugar treat, "Who's setting whom up, because if we're right, one of them could be next for the chop?"

Ant flicked a mint into his mouth and jumped to his feet.

"Time to revisit the crime scene. Come on, pull your wellies on. We're off to the boathouse."

"WILL you stop fiddling about with your nose," said Lyn as the pair hopped onto Geoff Singleton's boat and made their way into the cabin of the luxury cruiser.

Ant huffed as he gave his left nostril a final scratch

before settling himself down on a leather-covered bench seat next to the galley.

Lyn remained standing and scanned the immaculately fitted-out interior.

"What are we looking for?"

"I don't know until we find it, Lyn. I'm certain there's something here that will tell us what really happened. And if we're lucky, why he was killed."

There has to be something in here that will tell us what happened.

"It's not as if there's anywhere to hide anything, that's for sure," said Lyn as she opened various cupboards and inspected their interior.

Yes, got it!

Ant let out a triumphant cry and clapped his hands.

Lyn jumped at the sudden noise.

"What on earth's the matter with you. Have you gone mad?"

Ant beamed at her.

"You said it."

"Said what, Ant?"

"A hiding place."

He could see Lyn was none the wiser.

"Rufus, remember? He said Geoff had been very particular about wanting concealed storage in his new boat."

"And?"

"Well, if he wanted that kind of stuff in the new boat, it makes sense he's got one or two hidey-holes in this one. Don't you see?"

Lyn's changing body language told Ant his theory had clicked.

"So maybe he hid something in the cabin that his murderer wanted?"

Ant's smile broadened.

"Absolutely. All we have to do now is find it."

"If it's still here, Ant—whatever 'it' is."

Ten minutes passed. The banging of doors and knocking on timber panels became louder as their frustration grew.

"This is a waste of time," said Lyn as she knocked her knee on the corner of the dining table for the umpteenth time. "I've had enough; let's see if Jakub has anything else to say for himself. Perhaps he's been here?"

Just one more thing to try.

"Wait a minute." Ant pushed a narrow strip of wood under a low shelf, recessed to the point it was hidden from view. Straining to get a firm hold of the narrow facia, Ant first pressed then pulled the strip of teak. Nothing moved. In a final effort to prove his theory, Ant pushed the strip of wood upwards toward the shelf it was supposed to be supporting. Ant was rewarded by a satisfying "click."

"Yes."

"Have you found something, Ant?"

Now that the wood strip was free, he gently pulled it toward him.

"You can say that again."

Ant pulled the panel back to reveal a concealed compartment around three inches high and twelve inches deep.

"What's that?" asked Lyn as Ant removed a spiral-bound document of around fifty pages and glanced through the index page before quickly turning several pages, until he came across a table of figures.

"The reason Geoff Singleton was murdered, I suspect." He spoke slowly as he digested the mass of information.

Lyn strained to see what Ant was so engrossed in.

"Let me have a look."

Ant handed it over allowing Lyn to also scrutinise the figures. She shook her head, trying to make sense of the numbers.

"It's a new type of marine electric propulsion system, according to the title," said Lyn, "but it's not making any sense to me."

Ant moved closer so that they could both see the table of figures.

"Nor me. But Geoff certainly understood. See, look at his notes here, and here." Ant pointed to the pencil markings in the page margin.

"I think he discovered that whoever undertook the research into the new battery technology knew it didn't work then tried to massage the research results to hide the evidence."

It's as if his notes were meant for us.

"Perhaps he was about to go public."

Ant nodded at Lyn.

"Remember Rufus saying how Geoff always insisted on an ethical approach to business and his investment fund, Ant? What if these results compromised his reputation in some way?"

Ant's face lit up. Lyn's assessment sparked an idea.

"Who wrote the report?"

Ant gestured for Lyn to close the document and reveal the author's name on the front cover.

"Some outfit called EMGEN, Ant. And you know what? I've come across that name before."

15

NOSE TROUBLE

The centre of Stanton Parva was unusually quiet for a Saturday afternoon as Ant and Lyn sat on an old bench by the village pond. On the far side of the water, the Wherry Arms pub welcomed the occasional visitor, while the newsagent next door had to content itself with a delivery of soft drinks.

"I was reading the village magazine the other week. It seems we're not supposed to feed the ducks with bread," said Ant as he tossed the last of his wholemeal sandwich to a gaggle of wildfowl. The prospect of a free meal resulted in a terrific din as the birds scurried towards him to nab the best position.

"I read that too," replied Lyn as she watched the ducks being cheated of their treat by half a dozen seagulls, swooping down from the roof of a nearby thatched cottage. "I hate those things. If Phyllis Abbott and Betty didn't insist on feeding the things each day, they'd disappear back to the coast in a jiffy."

Ant did his best to wave the seagulls away. They were

having none of it. In protest, one left a chalky deposit on the shoulder of his coat.

"You're not the only one, I'd shoot the damn things if there wasn't a law against it. All I can say is, whichever civil servant in London came up with the ban has never had their clothes bleached by guano."

Ant glanced at Lyn just as what looked like a sympathetic smile dissolved into laugher.

"Oh, very funny," said Ant as he dabbed the glutinous white liquid from his coat.

"Don't be such a baby. It's a waxed jacket, isn't it? It'll wipe off easily enough."

Ant muttered a string of invective better suited to the army.

"Language, Ant."

He muttered some more as he focussed on the glint in Lyn's eye.

"That's not the point," he moaned as he gathered up the last of the guano with a paper tissue.

Ant watched as Lyn's smile turned to disdain.

"What?'

"What indeed, Ant. The tissue?"

Ant followed the tip of her index finger which was pointing at the scrunched-up mass in his right hand. He thought better of dropping the soggy tissue between the wooden slats of the bench. Instead, he trudged to a nearby waste bin before resuming his seat and glowering at the seagulls as they waited for the next titbit with a menacing look in their eyes.

"So," said Lyn as she encouraged a plain-coloured hen and its ducklings to move closer, while a more brightly coloured drake observed from a distance, "have you discovered anything else from the EMGEN report we found this morning?"

Ant stretched out his legs as if relaxing. In truth it was a tactic to discourage the wildfowl from getting any closer to him. Lyn's withering look soon made him change his mind.

"As a matter of fact, I think I have. It was something Dad said over lunch. He still dabbles in the stock market and has been tracking the performance of Geoff Singleton's investment fund; seems it specialised in investment for new technologies in the marine industry, which my father is still crazy about."

"Has he invested in Geoff?"

Ant shook his head.

"Now that would be a coincidence too far. No, it's just a hobby of his. Anyway, it turns out the report we found yesterday is the third in a series of updates produced for investors. Dad reckons that each time an update is released, which is, apparently, always more positive than the previous iteration, more people invest in his fund."

Lyn bent down to feed the hen. Ant wanted to shift the animal aside but decided discretion was the better part of valour.

"Let me guess, Ant. Once you've hyped the results once, you have to keep doing it. A small fib becomes a big lie, and so on."

Ant nodded.

"My guess is that once Geoff cottoned on to what was happening, it put him in a heck of a dilemma. Go public to save his reputation, or stay quiet and try to fix the problem —and keep his fortune."

Lyn shrugged her shoulders.

"Risky whichever way he jumped. Could the stress have brought on that heart attack?"

Ant raised an eyebrow.

"It's possible. But I guess if he was going to tell anyone he was in trouble, it would have been Hannah."

Lyn watched as the wildfowl deserted them for a new snack offered by a couple and their young child on the other side of the pond.

"I suppose she had a lot to lose as well. You know, brought up in poverty but enjoying all the trappings of wealth since meeting Geoff. Posh cars, fancy clothes, and the rest of it. I guess it would have been easy enough for her to bamboozle Jakub into bumping Geoff off before her world crashed?"

Ant rummaged in his jacket pocket as he digested Lyn's theory.

"Don't expect me to understand the workings of a woman's mind. I suppose the same might have applied to Geoff last Saturday. Perhaps he told her they were facing ruin. She hit the roof, so Geoff kept out of her way by re-varnishing his boat?"

Ant produced a tatty paper bag half full of manky-looking boiled sweets.

Lyn flinched as she peered into the discoloured bag.

"Just how long have you had those things in your pocket?"

Ant failed to understand the fuss she was making.

"Pear drops don't have a 'use-by' date. The trick is to keep them dry and away from daylight. Anyway, do you want one or not?"

Some people are really hard to please.

He watched as Lyn retrieved the cleanest-looking sweet she could find then spent several seconds picking it clean of fluff and bits of paper tissue.

Ant didn't bother to check the condition of his selection.

He sniffed the essence of the sweet by holding it close to his nostrils before popping the treat between his lips and sucking hard. His nostrils started to itch.

"For goodness' sake. What is it with you and those silly sweets? First you have a finger up your nose standing over Geoff at the boathouse, then you almost crash your precious Morgan scratching your snout."

Ignoring Lyn's protests, Ant wallowed in the fleeting pleasure of easing his itch, acutely aware of the pain which would follow.

Something clicked. It was if a light bulb had gone off in his head.

"What did you say?"

She gave him a puzzled look.

"Not to talk with your mouth full."

Ant shook his head, took the sweet from his mouth, and placed the sticky lozenge into his jacket pocket.

Lyn gave him a look that meant he was for the naughty chair had he been one of her pupils.

"No, no. You said *body* and *crash*."

Judging by the funny "ugh" sound Lyn was making, he knew she was still focussing on his eating habits.

"I think, Ant, that there were some other words in between those two that made my sentence grammatically correct, which is more than I can say for your conversational skills these days."

Ant's face lit up at his epiphany.

"And there we have it, Lyn."

"Have what?"

"How they did it and then skedaddled. Very clever. That is if my schoolboy chemistry is any good."

Lyn's bafflement continued as Ant sprang to his feet.

"I'm off to the boathouse. There's a couple of things I

need you to check while I have another shufti around. Give me a ring in about an hour, Lyn."

Ant stood in the eerie silence of the boathouse, with only the gentle wash of water audible as an occasional pleasure boat passed in front of the old wooden building. He knew exactly what he was looking for. Making his way into the cabin of Geoff's boat, he pulled open one of two exquisitely veneered cupboard doors beneath the stainless-steel sink.

Knew I'd seen it.

Ant retrieved a small paint brush. Opening the second door, his face lit up with a quiet sense of satisfaction as a bright steel tin, with its contents written on a lozenge-shaped, green paper label came into view:

Water-based Yacht Varnish
Wash brushes out in warm, clean water

He even used environmentally friendly varnish.

Ant imagined Geoff Singleton purposely making the decision to use the slower-drying liquid rather than a solvent-based alternative.

Picking up a dish cloth from the worktop, he lifted the tin from the cupboard and placed it onto the draining board.

Better keep my fingerprints off this.

Carefully, he levered the lid off the tin with a blunt knife and immediately felt his nostrils go into spasm.

An overpowering smell of pear drops filled the tiny cabin. It was too much. Ant quickly replaced the lid and ran for the open doors of the boathouse.

No water-based varnish gives off a vapour like that.

He gulped fresh oxygen like a blue whale scooping up krill. Just as his breathing began to settle, his mobile rang. He recognised the number as Lyn's.

"I've remembered where I saw the name EMGEN the other day. It was at Hannah's. I tried to get to her, but one of the neighbours said she'd seen her leave with Annabelle. Seems they drove away like a bat out of hell."

Ant wasted no time in responding.

"I'm certain now how Geoff was murdered. She's been very clever. Listen, stay there, and I'll pick you up on my way."

The line fell silent for a few seconds.

"To where?"

"See you in ten minutes. And ring Fitch for me, will you?" added Ant before briefing her on what to say to him. "And don't take no for an answer. Tell him there's two pints of Thatcher's Itch pale ale on me every night for a week, *if* he comes up trumps."

16

FLIGHT OF FANCY

Ant's Morgan roared down the A11 out of Norwich towards Cambridge taking little account of the speed limit.

"For goodness' sake, man, is she worth killing us both?"

Ant wasn't listening. His eyes focussed on a familiar shape in the distance as he pushed the sports car close to its limit. He couldn't make out the colour, but he knew it was a Range Rover 4 x 4.

"We'd better get Riley on the phone," said Ant, pointing to the mobile sitting in the centre console. Lyn did as he asked, and seconds later, a ringtone sounded through the car's speaker system.

Riley didn't bother with the usual pleasantries.

"And why exactly have you decided to interrupt my Saturday evening?"

Silence.

"Are you there? What is it you want?" The detective spoke in a loud, slow voice, articulating each syllable like a British holidaymaker in a foreign country.

Ant looked across to Lyn, who was glaring back at him.

"Enough, Ant."

He smiled.

"Good evening, Detective Inspector. How are you today?"

Ant could hear Riley trying to formulate a coherent response and assumed the detective's bad temper prevented him from doing so. Eventually he got the words out.

"I assume there is a point to your call?"

Ant dropped a gear as he engaged the car's right indicator, pressed the accelerator, and propelled the Morgan past a lorry with a full load of sugar beets.

"As a matter of fact, there is," replied Ant as he settled the Morgan back into the nearside lane.

Ant briefed him on developments, assisted by Lyn, who leant towards the car's microphone more than once to add details her co-sleuth had omitted.

"I didn't know you were so fond of me," said Ant as Lyn pressed into his side to make herself heard."

"Be assured that is most definitely not the case, Lord Stanton."

The two amateur detectives fell into a fit of laughter leaving Riley hanging on the phone until Ant had recovered sufficiently to respond.

"I'm hurt, Detective Inspector. Have you no feelings for me at all?"

Riley now knew he was having the rise taken out of him. Instead of trying to match Ant, he got down to the business at hand.

"So why haven't you said anything before now? I've warned you both before about withholding information from the police."

He's like a broken record.

"Because, Detective, until one hour ago, there was nothing to tell you other than a bunch of ideas Lyn and I had. Are you seriously telling me you'd have listened?" Ant's tone hardened. Gone was his "hail fellow, well met" persona. Now he spoke with the gravitas of a battle-hardened army intelligence officer. "One request, Detective Inspector Riley. Keep your traffic officers in their cages. I have no time to waste being pulled over and booked for speeding."

Ant didn't need to ask twice.

"You don't need to worry about that. Are you sure she's heading for the old airstrip at Fendham?"

Some common sense at last.

"No, but that's the direction she's driving in. I can't think where else she'd be going."

The mobile fell silent again, then Ant's car speaker rang out with the sound of a door being banged shut.

"I'm on my way now and about ten minutes behind you."

So he can make a decision when it suits him.

Twenty miles and fifteen minutes had elapsed since his call to Riley as Ant thundered along the A11. He could now see the 4 x 4's distinctive colour scheme, but not its occupants.

"Better ease back, Ant. We don't want her to see us."

Ant nodded and brought the Morgan back within the speed limit.

"Look out!" squealed Lyn as a roe deer jumped onto the carriageway from the thick field.

"Hellfire," shouted Ant as he caught a glimpse of the animal as it stopped and turned. Not knowing whether he had hit the beast or not, Ant struggled with the steering wheel to keep the vehicle upright and on the road.

Shouldn't have tried to avoid the stupid thing.

In a second it was over. Looking in his rear-view mirror, Ant could see the still outline of the deer as it looked aimlessly at the car from the safety of the grass verge.

"Damn those things. That was close." Adrenaline still surged through his body.

Lyn instinctively touched Ant's left arm and pressed gently to let him know it was okay.

"There's a lay-by up ahead. I'd better pull in and check for damage—and get my breath back."

Ant slowed, indicated, and brought the Morgan to a stop.

"It's that time of day, Ant. I hate driving early in the morning or sunset. It's like a scene from *Watership Down* around here sometimes with so many animals out and about."

Ant failed to hear Lyn's assessment of Norfolk wildlife. Instead, he gave the car one last check before clambering back into the Morgan.

"Lucky it turned just in time. Even though those things don't have any weight on them, they can still cause a right mess."

Lyn shook her head.

"Wouldn't have been particularly therapeutic for Bambi either, eh?"

Ant was already back on the hunt for the 4 x 4, dismissing Lyn's observation with a grunt.

"We're losing the light, and they've disappeared, damn it," said Ant as the Morgan shot back onto the carriageway and sped towards Cambridge. "This is hopeless. Listen, give Riley a ring and see if he can give us directions."

Lyn grabbed Ant's mobile and tapped in the detective's number, looked across to Ant, and waited for Riley to respond.

"Blast it, the signal's dropped out."

Ant's attention was suddenly elsewhere. He let out a sudden whoop of excitement, making Lyn jump.

"Doesn't matter, there she blows." He pointed towards a clump of trees to their right about a mile ahead.

"What?"

"Laser light. That green thing. Can't you see it?"

Now that she knew what she was looking for, it stood out like a sore thumb.

"Good heavens. Riley said some kids had been using a laser light to distract local aircraft, except—"

"Except," interrupted Ant, "we're not talking about kids distracting the pilot, are we? If I'm right, whoever is holding that light is doing the exact opposite."

Lyn nodded.

"So she's guiding an aircraft onto the old landing strip. Tricky to land on something that was last used in 1945?"

Ant smiled as he took a right turn across the carriageway and propelled the Morgan up a dusty trackway. Ahead, lay a small gap in a thick clump of trees.

"I guess if you're desperate enough, you'll try anything." Ant turned the Morgan's engine and headlights off and allowed the car to coast to a stop.

"Come on, Lyn. Quietly does it. Stay within the treeline with me, so we can get as close as possible without spooking them. We need that plane to land."

Ant put his military training to good use as he navigated through the close columns of pine trees that held sentinel between friend and foe.

"I can see them," whispered Lyn. "Look, over there."

Slowly, slowly does it.

Barely twenty feet now stood between them and two women, their backs to Ant and Lyn, with one holding a laser pen pointing to the star-filled night sky.

One more push.

Ant signalled for Lyn to stay close as they crept forward and closed the final few yards.

"Good evening, ladies."

Hannah and Annabelle visibly jumped and look stunned as they turned from the rear corner of the Range Rover to face the intruders.

Got you.

"You took some catching," said Lyn.

Hannah attempted to distract Lyn, while Annabelle pointed a pen-like laser back into the darkening sky.

Ant ignored the woman's actions as he inspected the front of the 4 x 4. He found what he expected. The corner of the vehicle showed signs of damage with paint residue etched into its surface.

Hannah looked at Annabelle, who continued to scour the sky for signs of an aircraft. Her face lit up as she caught a first glimpse of a moving light in the heavens. Ant noted Annabelle was pointing the laser slightly below its source.

Don't want to blind the pilot, do we?

Seconds later, a four-seater plane touched down on a short strip of concrete that had remained intact from its wartime use. The plane's propeller was still running with the engine over-revving.

Not the first time he's done a quick turnaround.

He turned to Hannah, who wore a look of desperation.

"It's my only chance. The police blame me for stealing Geoff's body. They think I murdered my husband. Annabelle has arranged all this for me. Please, let us go."

Before either Ant or Lyn could respond, the two women ran towards the aircraft's open passenger door and started to clamber aboard.

As Ant chased after them, the sound of a police car siren

outdid the roar of the plane's engines as it turned and started to taxi. Its progress was halted as Riley's car pulled up a short distance in front of the plane, effectively blocking any escape.

Detective Inspector Riley sprang from his police Jaguar.

"So you were right," he said to Ant as the policeman pulled open the passenger door, shouted at the pilot to cut the engine, and peered inside at the two passengers.

"Hannah Singleton, I arrest you for the murder of—"

Ant interrupted Riley as Hannah looked forlornly at the floor.

"It wasn't Hannah, Detective Inspector. Annabelle Emms murdered Geoff Singleton." Ant's voice lacked any sign of emotion as he glared at Annabelle.

Riley frowned.

"You said—"

"I," interrupted Ant, "said *she* was responsible, and that I could prove it. I didn't say *which* of them murdered Mr Singleton."

Hannah protested as Riley ordered both women to leave the plane.

"No, no. You have it wrong. Annabelle is helping me to escape. She did not kill my husband. Why would she?"

Annabelle's shocked look reinforced Hannah's plea.

Ant allowed stillness to descend. For a few seconds, the only sound came from leaves rustling in the light breeze of a cool evening.

"We were all together in the pub garden the day Geoff died. How could I have anything to do with the death of my dearest friend?"

Who's the cool one, then?

Ant smiled.

"Geoffrey had a heart problem; everyone knew that," Annabelle continued. "Hannah knows what happened. His heart gave out, just like his uncle. Why do you make these things worse for her? You are a cruel man."

Ant noticed Riley giving him a stern look and guessed he had no intention of being made to look a fool again.

"Correct on both counts."

Annabelle started to smile.

"But," Ant continued, "there are many ways to make a heart stop. Sometimes the body does this itself. Other times something is done to make it stop. And that's what you did, wasn't it, Annabelle?"

Ant looked deep into her eyes to determine if his hypothesis held up. Hannah shook her head.

"No, no... you are wrong, mad."

Lyn held out a hand to Hannah.

"I've told you. I was at the BBQ. You saw me. Jakub must have killed Geoff. I told you how jealous he was and that I'd seen him in the village."

"Ah, yes. Well, I spoke to that gentleman. He maintains Hannah rang him to say she needed his help."

Hannah pulled away from Lyn.

"I did not speak to him. Why would I do this?"

Riley's neck swivelled from side to side like a spectator at a Wimbledon tennis final.

Ant changed tack.

"Is that your Range Rover, Annabelle?"

"What are you talking about?" she replied as she turned to look at the aircraft.

"It's okay, Annabelle. I've already checked. The car is yours. Unfortunately for you, you hit a car in your haste to get away from the boathouse after you placed chloral hydrate into the tin of varnish Geoff was using to spruce up his boat before selling it."

"Chloral hydrate?"

Ant ignored the policeman's parrot-like repetition.

"You see, Annabelle, pear drops make my nose itch. Isn't that right, Lyn?"

Lyn nodded, her amusement obvious for all to see.

"And as it turns out, chloral hydrate also smells of pear drops. Lucky, really. Well, perhaps not for you." Ant moved closer to Annabelle to press home his dominance of the space between them.

"You don't have any proof of this nonsense. You are just making this up."

You can look as angry as you like, lady.

"Oh, I think I have. I'm sure your fingerprints will be all over that can. You got sloppy, Annabelle. Were you running out of time to pick Hannah up and get to the BBQ? I think you were, so you couldn't get the tin away from Geoff after you spiked it, to get rid of your fingerprints. Or perhaps you just assumed the police would think he died of natural causes, and you didn't need to bother. After all, poor Geoff would have innocently used the varnish then put the tin away. He was tidy like that, wasn't he? All the time he was in that cabin, the fumes were doing their work; Geoff was unaware it was killing him. I assume you knew he had a poor sense of smell, so he didn't notice anything wrong. In the end, he just sat down and died—but only because you poisoned him."

Annabelle stood rooted to the spot.

Hannah's gaze burned into her.

The temporary silence was broken by a ringtone.

"I think that's for you, Annabelle."

Annabelle looked at Lyn, then the handset gave off an eerie halo in the darkness.

Lyn held up a second handset, its screen also illuminated.

"This is Jakub's phone, Annabelle. You know, the one you rang to get him over from Poland. The one you dialled to fool him it was Hannah ringing, and the one you used to get him to move Geoff's body."

Hannah cried out as if in physical pain. Lyn walked her away from the group, giving what comfort she could from the relative quiet of Ant's car.

Ant noticed Annabelle's demeanour change. When Fitch pulled up with Jakub in tow, it broke completely.

Almost there.

"That report was written by your husband's research company, wasn't it?"

Annabelle gave the faintest of nods to acknowledge Ant's question.

"Geoff told you he'd realised what had been going on, and that he wasn't prepared to ruin his reputation. He realised your husband had got his findings wrong, yes?"

A tear rolled down Annabelle's cheek.

"My husband knows nothing of what I have done. We would have been ruined. Twenty years of work gone in a second, along with everything we own."

Riley started to move forward holding a pair of handcuffs in his right hand.

"I told Geoff we could fix things. He didn't believe me. He said one lie would lead to another and he couldn't allow that. Well, I couldn't let him ruin us."

Ant took a step away from Annabelle.

"And so you did your own research. You found out chloral hydrate had been used as a sedative, but if administered in a big enough dose, it could stop the heart, especially where a weakness already existed."

Annabelle nodded again. The rest of her body hung limp.

"Pretending to be Hannah to ensure Jakub came was a clever touch, I'll give you that. As was arranging for me to be pulled over by that bogus copper. One day I'll find out who told you so much about me to make it so convincing. And who knows, if my mate, Fitch, hadn't been called out to fix a generator, Geoff's body would have vanished forever. Hey, presto, no autopsy results to show traces of chloral hydrate. Just Hannah's spurned lover with a history of violence.

"But you got sloppy when you gave me all that guff about buying the old chapel and having to fly back to Poland to sort out your finances. Did you not think I would check with the estate agent? It took us five minutes to discover the building wasn't for sale after all. Instead, it was Jakub you had just met when I came across you on Wednesday, wasn't it? As for your flight, well, you never left the country, did you?"

Annabelle sobbed and gazed down at the leaf-strewn concrete without answering.

"Over to you, Detective Inspector." Ant vacated the scene and turned to see Jakub leaning into the open-topped Morgan. His arm provided a protective blanket around Hannah's shoulders as they exchanged warm smiles.

"Oh, I have something for you, my Polish friend."

Jakub turned towards Ant.

"A certain young lady asked that I give you this." Ant held out the change Lil had given him for Jakub. "I know food is expensive in the UK, but even we don't charge twenty pounds for a burger!"

Nice to see you smile.

"You did say two pints of Thatcher's Itch every night for a

week, my Lord Stanton?" Fitch reinforced his point by pointing at the wooden beer pump handle at the bar of the Wherry Inn.

"Yes, he did," interjected Lyn.

I give up.

Ant reached into his trouser pocket to retrieve his wallet.

"Watch out for the moths," quipped Fitch.

"Very funny," replied Ant as he drew the attention of the barman and handed over 5 twenty-pound notes. "Put this behind the bar for my friend. If there's anything left by the end of the week, pop it into the lifeboat collection box. Never let it be said I don't pay my debts."

Ant was amused to watch Fitch and Lyn exchange confused glances knowing shelling out cash was not something either of them were used to seeing him do that often.

"What are you up to?"

Ant looked furtively at Fitch as he shuffled from one foot to another.

"As a matter of fact, I need a favour."

"I knew it," moaned Fitch.

"Out with it," demanded Lyn.

Ant played for time by taking a large gulp of his Fen Bodger pale ale.

"I came across a couple of teenagers stripping lead off Hill Rise Folly earlier in the week. The upshot is I said I might be able to help them find a job."

Don't look so suspicious, Fitch.

"What, as plumbers, or demolition experts?"

Having just taken a gulp from her glass, Lyn laughed then coughed as the bubbles from her white wine spritzer hit the back of her nose.

"Er, not exactly. The lad wants to work with animals, so I got him a placement with the vet."

"And the other one." Ant hesitated as Fitch's eyes narrowed.

"She wants to be a mechanic."

Fitch froze.

"*She*—a mechanic? Don't tell me you—"

Ant looked nervously towards the pub's front door then ran.

"I've told her to pop along to the garage first thing on Monday. Is that okay?"

Fitch was up in a flash.

"Lord or not, you come back here before I…"

END

GLOSSARY

English (UK) to US English

- **A rum do:** A strange or surprising occurrence
- **Bakelite:** Early type of plastic
- **Boiled sweet:** Candy mainly made from sugar and flavourings boiled into a hard treat
- **Bonce:** Street slang for head. "I hit my bonce on the shelf."
- **Broad:** A stretch of shallow water formed from old peat diggings. Common in Norfolk and Suffolk regions of the UK. Can take the form of narrow stretches of water like canals, or open water like small lakes.
- **Car boot:** Trunk
- **Cottoned on:** Finally understood something
- **Fobbed off:** Street slang for not being taken seriously
- **Folly:** A building with no practical use. Traditionally constructed by wealthy landowners on their estate as a symbol of their power and

prestige. Can be a simple tower or obelisk, or more ornate faux castle ruin, for example.
- **Gawping:** Old-fashioned English word for looking obtrusively at something or (more usually) someone
- **Gurning:** A traditional British pastime in which individuals pull a grotesque face by projecting the lower jaw as far forward as possible then covering the upper lip with the lower lip. The head of the competitor is usually placed through a horse's harness as a "frame"
- **Jiffy:** A word to describe doing something almost immediately—"I'll be with you in a jiffy."
- **Lay-by:** A safe place to park at the side of a highway
- **Holby City:** Eponymous UK soap opera based in a hospital
- **Manky:** Something, or someone, who smells of a bad odour. Often used to describe something that is falling to bits
- **Mackintosh:** A eponymous waterproof coat or jacket
- **Newsagent:** A shop which sells newspapers, magazines, tobacco and candy
- **Plod:** nickname for a policeman or "the police"
- **Pillar box:** A Royal Mail postal box sited in public places and usually painted bright red (pillar-box red)
- **Quid:** Pound sterling
- **Shandy:** A mixture of roughly 50% or more of beer and 50% lemonade (soda)
- **Shufti:** Street slang used to describe having a look at something. Often said in jest

- **Sixpence:** A UK coin used until 1971 and worth approximately two US cents today
- **Snug:** A small room in an English pub. Old-fashioned and not designed for pubs today
- **That's the ticket:** Showing courage or willing to do something with a good heart
- **The City:** London's financial district and stock exchange
- **Tight:** Does not spend money easily—penny-pincher
- **Toad-in-the-hole:** British food dish first described in 1762 as a pastry dish containing a small piece of beef. Used to make meat go further in poor households
- **Toerag:** Street slang to describe someone who cannot be trusted
- **Toff:** Slang word for upper-class or rich person generally seen to be "looking down" on other people
- **Turned on a sixpence:** turned on the spot
- **Trolley:** A gurney used in hospitals
- **Wherry:** A traditional sailboat used for carrying goods and passengers on the Norfolk & Suffolk Broads
- **You're a corker:** Old-fashioned description of something excellent in a thing or person

DID YOU ENJOY THE BOATHOUSE KILLER?

Reviews are so important in helping get my books noticed. Unlike the big, established authors and publishers, I don't have the resources available for big marketing campaigns and expensive book launches (though I live in hope!).

What I *do* have, gratefully, is the following of a loyal and growing band of readers.

Genuine reviews of my writing help bring my books to the attention of new readers.

If you enjoyed this book, it would be a great help if you could spare a couple of minutes and kindly head over to my Amazon page to leave a review (as short or long as you like). All you need do is click on one of the links, below.
    UK
    US

Thank you so much.

JOIN MY READERS' CLUB

Getting to know my readers is the thing I like most about writing. From time to time I publish a newsletter with details on my new releases, special offers, and other bits of news relating to the Norfolk Murder Mystery series. If you join my Readers' Club, I'll send you this gripping short story free and ONLY available to club members:

A Record of Deceit: 17,000 word short story

Grace Pinfold is terrified a stranger wants to kill her. Disturbing phone calls and mysterious letters confirm the threat is real. Then Grace disappears. Ant and Lyn fear they have less than forty-eight hours to find Grace before tragedy strikes - a situation made worse by a disinterested Detective Inspector Riley who's convinced an innocent explanation exists.

Character Backgrounds: A 7,000 word insight

Read fascinating interviews with the four lead characters in the Norfolk Cozy Mysteries series. Anthony Stanton, Lyn Blackthorn, Detective Inspector Riley and Fitch explain what drives them, their backgrounds and let slip an insight into each of their characters. We also learn how Ant, Lyn and Fitch first met as children and grew up to be firm friends - even if they do drive each other crazy most of the time!

You can get your free content by visiting my website at www.keithjfinney.com

I look forward to seeing you there.

Keith

For Joan who is always there for me.

ACKNOWLEDGMENTS

Cover design by Books Covered

Edit & Proofreading: Paula.
paulaproofreader.wixsite.com/home

ALSO BY KEITH FINNEY

In the Norfolk Murder Mystery Series:

Dead Man's Trench

Narky Collins, Stanton Parva's most hated resident lies dead at the bottom of an excavation trench. Was it an accident, or murder?

Amateur sleuths, Ant and Lyn, team up to untangle a jumble of leads as they try to discover the truth when jealousy, greed, and blackmail combine into an explosive mix of lies and betrayal.

Will the investigative duo succeed, or fall foul of Detective Inspector Riley?

Murder by Hanging

Ethan Baldwin, a respected resident of Stanton Parva, hangs from a tree in the woods on the edge of the village. Detective Inspector Riley thinks it's suicide. Ant and Lyn are sure he's been murdered. But who would want to kill the church warden?

www.keithjfinney.com

FACEBOOK

PUBLISHED BY:
Norfolk Cozy Mystery Publishing
Copyright © 2020

All rights reserved.

No part of this publication may be copied, reproduced in any format, by any means, electronic or otherwise, without prior consent from the copyright owner and publisher of this book.

This is a work of fiction. All characters, names, including business or building names are the product of the author's imagination Any resemblance that any of the above bear to real businesses is coincidental.

www.keithjfinney.com

❀ Created with Vellum

Printed in Great Britain
by Amazon